TRIPLE HEADER

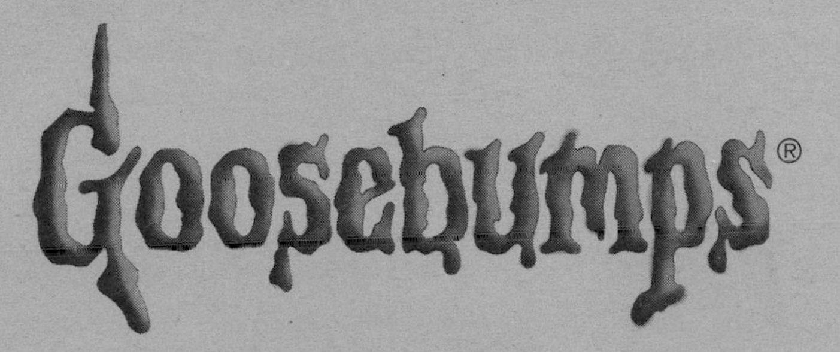

R.L. STINE

THREE SHOCKING TALES OF TERROR

——— Book 2 ———

Look for more Goosebumps Series 2000
by R.L. Stine:

#1 Cry of the Cat
#2 Bride of the Living Dummy
#3 Creature Teacher
#4 Invasion of the Body Squeezers (Part I)
#5 Invasion of the Body Squeezers (Part II)

TRIPLE HEADER

Goosebumps®

R.L. STINE

THREE SHOCKING TALES OF TERROR

Book 2

SCHOLASTIC INC.
New York Toronto London Auckland Sydney

A PARACHUTE PRESS BOOK

ISBN 0-590-76252-4

12 11 10 9 8 7 6 5 4 3 2 1 8 9/9 0 1 2 3/0

Printed in the U.S.A. 40

First Scholastic printing, May 1998

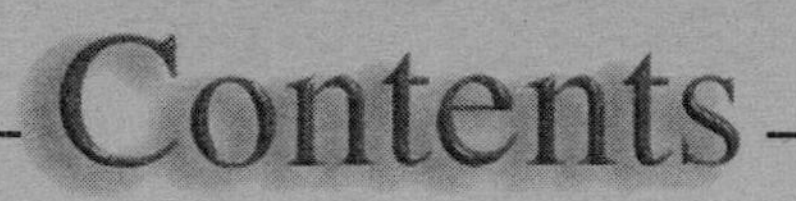

Welcome to Triple Terror

SLIM: Hello, boys and ghouls. Welcome to this Goosebumps Triple Header. I'm a triple header too. My name is Slim, and I'm the good-looking one in the middle. I'm the *head*master around here.

LEFTY: How'd you get to be Triple Header headmaster? You can't even count to three!

SLIM: Yes, I can. It's easy. I just count all my fingers and subtract twenty-seven!

RIGHTY: I could do that — if I didn't eat the calculator. Why can't I be headmaster?

SLIM: You're ugly and you smell bad.

RIGHTY: I *know* my good qualities. I asked you what's *wrong* with me!

LEFTY: Hey — I smell a *lot* worse than he does!

SLIM: There you go, bragging again. I

want to brag about our stories. Every Goosebumps Triple Header has three stories — three times the scares. I hope you'll collect them all.

RIGHTY: All you collect is *flies*!

SLIM: (sigh) People ask me if it's difficult having three heads.

LEFTY: What do you tell them?

SLIM: Yes, no, and maybe . . .

Ghoul School

Introduction

LEFTY: Hey, I had a talk with my teacher today. She said I was smart, nice, and well behaved.

SLIM: Don't feel bad. You'll do better *next* semester!

LEFTY: Righty, I hear you flunked math.

RIGHTY: Yeah. Do you know why?

LEFTY: Why?

RIGHTY: I subtracted the teacher!

SLIM: That brings us to our first story. It's called "Ghoul School." It's about a kid named Liam who finds himself going to a school full of ugly, terrifying, hungry monsters.

LEFTY: Lucky guy!

1

Twenty pairs of eyes stared at me as I walked into the classroom.

It was October and my first day at a new school. I was a new kid. And I was late. So even though I'm a pretty normal-looking guy — brown eyes, brown hair — I expected stares.

But I didn't expect a stare like the one I got from the chubby kid at the desk by the door. His bulging eyes were swamp-green — all over. Even the white parts seemed sort of green.

Weird! I glanced away.

I shouldn't have done that.

That's when I spotted a girl staring at me. She had regular brown eyes. But her mouth hung open. A slimy river of drool poured over her bottom lip. The drool hit her desk. *SPLAT!*

Yuck!

I glanced at my note from the school secretary. It said I was to go to Room 5. But this couldn't be right. I must be in the wrong room. I stepped back and checked the number on the door.

Room 5.

I was in the right room.

But something seemed very wrong here.

A tall girl stood beside an aquarium. She glanced back at me as she licked the wall.

Standing next to her was a blond girl with braids. She glared at me while she chewed on the end of her ruler.

Ugh! These kids were so gross!

The teacher sat at her desk, reading. Totally ignoring her drooling, ruler-chewing students.

I made my way over to her. "Um, excuse me," I said.

She glanced up and smiled. "Yes?"

I let out a sigh of relief. My new teacher looked nice and friendly. And *normal*. Her brown hair was cut short, and she wore round glasses on the tip of her nose.

"I'm Liam Erdman," I told her. "My family just moved here."

"Welcome to Room 5, Liam," the teacher said. "I'm Ms. Barker. Take a seat over there."

She pointed to an empty desk in the second row, behind the wall licker.

"Okay." I walked over to the desk and sat down.

Then Ms. Barker asked all the kids to tell me their names.

"Bernard," the boy with the big weird eyes called out.

"Rachel," the drooler mumbled.

The tall girl stopped licking the wall. "Susan!" she shouted shrilly. Then she sat down and started licking her desk.

"Helga," the ruler chewer snapped.

The kids all told me their names. And every kid seemed strange in some way.

I wish I was still at my old school, I thought. How am I going to make it through the year with these weirdos?

"Math time," Ms. Barker announced. "First row, go to the chalkboard."

Bernard went up with the first group. Ms. Barker gave a word problem. Bernard picked up a stick of chalk — and tossed it into his mouth.

"The chalk, Bernard!" Ms. Barker said sharply.

Bernard grinned sheepishly. Then he choked

and sputtered and coughed up one very slimy stick of chalk. He began to write.

"Oh, man!" I gasped.

I was in the next group. I walked up to the board. Bernard held out his chalk to me. Spit dripped off it.

I jumped back. "Ugh!"

Bernard scowled.

"I mean, no thanks, Bernard," I managed. I grabbed a clean stick of chalk from the chalk tray.

Bernard shrugged and popped his chalk back into his mouth. I heard him chewing it as he went back to his seat.

I stared hard at Ms. Barker. But she didn't say a word.

It seemed like hours before Ms. Barker called, "Lunchtime! The front two rows may go first."

I hurried out of the classroom with the others. I followed them down the stairs to the cafeteria.

I took a burger with fries and a milk. Then I carried my tray over to a table on the far side of the cafeteria.

A boy was sitting at the table already. He wore a dog collar around his neck. But compared to the kids in Room 5, he seemed pretty normal.

No drooling. No bulging eyes. I sat across from him.

The boy stared at me for a second. "You're new here, aren't you?" he said in a low voice.

I nodded as I lifted my burger to my mouth.

"Don't *do* that!" the boy ordered sharply.

"Huh? Don't do what?" I asked.

"Your elbows. Don't *ever* stick them out like that," he warned. "Keep your arms and hands close to your body."

"Okay." I brought in my elbows. "But why?"

The boy shrugged. "You'll see."

What was *that* supposed to mean?

As I picked up my burger again, I heard a roar. I turned to see the rest of Room 5 stampeding into the cafeteria. The kids screamed and yelled and shoved each other.

They didn't even bother taking trays. Or plates. They simply grabbed food and crammed it into their mouths.

"What a bunch of animals!" I muttered. Being in Room 5 was the worst thing that had ever happened to me!

Susan ran past me, waving a burger in each hand. A third burger stuck out of her mouth.

Bernard chased after her, screaming, "Burger thief!"

The dog-collar boy across the table from me started *barking*!

Then he jumped up and raced after Bernard — on all fours!

All I could do was stare.

Rachel whirled around to face Bernard. She spit a mouthful of chewed-up hamburger at him. Bernard quickly dropped to his hands and knees. He and the dog-collar boy started gobbling up the half-chewed burger from the cafeteria floor.

"Oh, yuck!" I cried. I tossed my burger onto my plate.

I wasn't hungry anymore. My appetite was gone.

A second later, so was my burger. Susan had struck again. She stood above me, shrieking and licking the bun.

My stomach lurched. I felt sick! Pushing back my chair, I bolted for the door.

I zoomed by the table where Helga and Rachel were sitting. Helga stuck out her foot.

BAM! I tripped and slid across the cafeteria floor on my stomach. When I finally stopped, I shut my eyes and lay still for a second, trying to catch my breath.

That's when I heard growling right above my head.

I opened my eyes — and gasped.

Helga stood over me, growling and gnashing little pointy teeth. Rachel lurked behind her, drooling up a storm.

"I'm hungry," Helga grunted. "Hungry!"

She lifted my arm.

And opened her mouth wide to take a bite.

2

"No!" I screamed. I jerked my arm away from Helga. My heart pounded with fear.

Helga growled.

Rachel gurgled.

They were closing in on me.

I had to escape!

Quickly, I rolled away from my attackers. I scrambled to my feet and took off running. I didn't stop until I reached Room 5. I yanked open the door and ran inside.

The teacher sat at her desk, unwrapping a sandwich.

I'd never been so glad to see anyone in my life!

"Ms. Barker!" I cried as I ran toward her.

Ms. Barker stopped unwrapping her sandwich and glanced up. "Yes, Liam?"

I stood beside her desk, panting. "The kids . . ." I managed at last. "The ones in this class. They . . . they act like *monsters*!"

Ms. Barker nodded. "They certainly do."

"But . . . but can't you *do* something?" I asked her. "Can't you get them to stop?"

"I don't see how," Ms. Barker said, shrugging. "They're behaving just the way they're supposed to."

I stared at her. "What do you mean?"

Ms. Barker frowned. "Didn't your parents tell you?"

"Tell me what?" I asked.

"This is a *ghoul school,* Liam," she replied calmly. "The students here *are* monsters."

A *ghoul school*?

"Not me!" I cried. "I'm not a monster!"

"Shhhh!" Ms. Barker put a finger to her lips. "Don't say that, Liam! Don't let the other students know."

"Why not?" I demanded.

"If they find out you aren't a monster . . ." Ms. Barker's voice trailed off, and she shook her head. "Well, I don't know *what* they'll do, Liam. But, trust me — you won't like it."

A high squeak of terror escaped from my lips.

"I don't belong here!" I moaned. "I have to go home!"

Ms. Barker shook her head. "You do belong here. I checked your records this morning," she told me. "Your parents asked that you be placed in this school."

"No! There must be a mistake!" I cried. "They'd never send me to a ghoul school!"

"Speak to your parents tonight," Ms. Barker advised. "But in the meantime, be careful. And I mean *careful.*" She shook her head again. "These kids are really dangerous."

I swallowed. This was a nightmare!

"Don't let them know you're not a monster," Ms. Barker warned again. "And whatever you do," she added, "don't let them see that you're afraid."

"Okay," I squeaked. "No problem."

I wasn't afraid.

I was scared to death!

"Go on outside now," Ms. Barker said. "I need a few minutes to eat my ham sandwich. Do what I said, Liam, and you'll be fine."

My legs shook as I walked out of Room 5. Ms. Barker's words echoed inside my head. *These kids are really dangerous.*

I walked slowly to the front door of the school. I pushed the door partway open and peeked out into the playground.

I saw Susan. She was licking the jungle gym.

Bernard jumped up and down on a flattened soccer ball.

Helga stood off by herself. She had her ruler with her. She was chewing it to shreds! She made low, growling sounds as her pointy little teeth ripped into the wood.

I shuddered. That's what Helga tried to do to my arm!

I wanted to run back to Room 5. I wanted to disappear!

But Ms. Barker said I had to go out there. To show them I wasn't afraid.

I drew a breath. Then I pushed the door open all the way and stepped outside.

Instantly, all the kids on the playground stopped doing what they were doing. They stared at me.

They know! I told myself. They know I'm not a monster. They know I'm afraid! And they're going to get me!

"Oh, I forgot to bring out my . . . uh, my baseball bat," I mumbled. "I think I'll go get it."

I backed up to the door. No way was I turning my back on those monsters!

Helga spit out a chunk of her ruler. "A baseball bat!" she exclaimed. "I *love* baseball bats!"

I jerked open the door and charged back inside. Maybe if I begged Ms. Barker, she'd let me stay in.

My hand was shaking as I opened the door of Room 5. Ms. Barker sat at her desk, eating her ham sandwich.

I opened my mouth to call her name.

But my voice stuck in my throat. I couldn't say anything.

All I could do was stare at Ms. Barker's sandwich.

3

Thick, blue fingers stuck out from between two slices of bread. The fingers had long red fingernails.

Ms. Barker brought the sandwich up to her lips. Then she opened her mouth and bit into it. Bones crunched between her teeth. She made a ghastly gulping sound as she swallowed.

My eyes opened wide in horror.

Ms. Barker wasn't eating a ham sandwich.

She was eating a *hand* sandwich.

My teacher was a monster too!

Slowly I backed out of Room 5.

I eased the door shut behind me.

I had to get out of this school!

I sprinted down the hallway toward the back door. A red Exit sign hung over the door. That was *exactly* what I wanted!

I ran to the door and pushed it open.

I was free!

Except that in front of me stood a brick wall. It was ten feet high. It had barbed wire at the top.

I ran along the wall, searching desperately for a gate. Searching for some way out of this place.

But there was no gate. I was trapped!

My stomach knotted in fear as I walked back into the school. There was only one way out. And that was through the front door. Through the playground. The monsters' playground.

And I knew I'd never make it past those kids alive.

I ducked into the boys' room. I sat in a stall for a few minutes, trying to think out my problem.

I was the only normal kid at a monster school.

The monsters were really dangerous.

I was really scared.

Finally I decided there was only one thing to do.

I had to pretend that everything was okay.

I had to forget that I had seen Ms. Barker munching on a hand.

Most important of all, I had to act like a monster myself.

When I heard the other kids come in from recess, I took a deep breath. Then I walked out of the boys' room and into Room 5.

Helga pounced on me as I came through the door.

"Baseball bat!" she growled. She gnashed her pointy teeth at me. "I want a bite!"

"I ate it myself!" I growled. Then I dashed for my desk.

I don't know how I made it through the afternoon. For science, Ms. Barker led a class discussion on rabies. In art, we painted. But there was only one color of paint — bloodred.

At the end of the day, Ms. Barker read us a chapter of *How to Eat Fried Worms*. It's a funny book. But nobody in Room 5 laughed. They all just smacked their lips and drooled every time Ms. Barker said the word "worm."

It was a *long* afternoon.

"Mom!" I cried when she came home from work that afternoon.

"Help me with these groceries, Liam." She handed me a bag.

I hurried after her into the kitchen. I set the

bag down on the counter. "Mom, my new school is *horrible*!" I wailed.

Mom started putting away the groceries.

"It's full of monsters, Mom," I blurted out. "I'm not making this up. The kids in my class chew their rulers to bits and lick the walls. In the cafeteria, they spit out chewed-up food, and other kids gobble it up off the floor."

Mom kept putting away the groceries. "Well, you'll have to set a good example for them, Liam," she said. "Show them what it's like to have good manners."

"This isn't about manners!" I cried.

The door from the garage opened, and my dad walked into the kitchen. He's an undercover policeman. It sounds exciting, but it isn't. He works at a mall, checking for shoplifters.

"Dad!" I cried. "My new school! It's full of monsters!"

Dad glanced at Mom.

Mom shrugged. "Liam says the kids act like monsters."

"They don't *act like* monsters!" I yelled. "They *are* monsters! The teacher even said so. She said it's a ghoul school. That everybody in it is a monster. Everybody but *me*."

"She was obviously joking, Liam," Dad told me. "She must have a strange sense of humor."

"She's strange, all right," I agreed. I told them about Ms. Barker's lunch.

"Oh, Liam!" Mom sighed. "Your imagination is running wild. As soon as you make a friend, everything will be much better."

I rolled my eyes. I could just picture Helga and me stopping off at the Unpainted Furniture Store for a bite.

I followed my dad into his study. He sat down at his desk and began sorting through a stack of papers.

"Dad, my teacher says that you wanted me to be in this school," I said. "Is that true?"

Dad put down the papers. "It's the closest school, Liam," he pointed out. "You'd have to take a long bus ride to any other school. Give it a couple of weeks. Then, if you still don't like it, you can switch to another school."

"There's only one problem with that plan," I told him. "I won't be alive in two weeks!"

Dad frowned. "I guess the kids at your new school are tougher than the kids you're used to."

"Right," I agreed gloomily. "None of the kids at my old school ever tried to take a bite out of my arm."

Dad sighed. "I think you're exaggerating, Liam. But I tell you what. How about if I give you a special police protection device?" He opened one of his desk drawers and pulled out a tiny silver button.

"This is a safety button," he told me. "Put it in your shirt pocket tomorrow. If you get really scared, press the button. But do me a favor. Don't use it unless it's a *real* emergency."

I took the silver button from him. It was smaller than a wristwatch battery. It sure didn't look like much.

"How?" I asked. "How can such a little thing protect me?"

"It's too complicated to explain," Dad said. He herded me toward the study door. "I've got a lot of paperwork to get through. See you later, all right?"

"But —" I protested, turning back toward him.

Dad closed the door in my face.

The next morning, I told Mom I had a fever. "I'm pretty sure I'm coming down with something awful."

Mom leaned over and felt my forehead.

"Have fun at school, Liam," she said with a smile.

Sighing, I got dressed. I dropped the tiny safety button into my shirt pocket. Then I walked slowly to school.

When I reached the playground, Helga and Bernard ran up to me. Helga had dirt smears all around her mouth. She clutched more dirt in both fists.

Bernard pushed me. His buggy eyes spun in their sockets. He kept pushing until I was backed up against the playground fence.

"Cut it out!" I ordered. I tried to keep my voice from shaking.

Staring at me, Helga brought a hand to her mouth. She started gobbling up the dirt with horrible snorting noises.

I thought I was going to lose my breakfast on the spot.

When Helga finished, she licked the dirt off her palm. She grinned at me. Dirt was caked between her pointy teeth.

She held out the other hand full of dirt to me.

"Eat it," she growled.

"Uh, no thanks," I mumbled. "I already had breakfast."

"Eat it!" Bernard yelled. "EAT IT! EAT IT!" His eyes bulged so much, I thought they might pop out of his head.

Rachel and Susan ran over. "What are you yelling about?" Rachel demanded.

"He won't eat dirt!" Bernard snarled.

"Eat it!" Rachel ordered. "Go on!" Spit flowed over her chin. Her T-shirt was sopping wet.

"I said *no*!" I yelled. "Why are you giving me a hard time?"

"We don't believe you're a monster," Bernard growled.

"What?" I tried to sound outraged. "Of *course* I am!"

Rachel made a gurgling sound. I think it was a laugh.

"No, you're not!" Susan shrieked.

"I am too," I insisted. "Only monsters are allowed at this school. I go here. So I must be a monster."

Bernard stepped closer to me. "If you're a monster," he croaked, "then prove it."

"Prove it!" Susan screamed.

"Prove it!" Rachel gurgled.

"Yeah," Helga growled. "Prove it — *or else*!"

4

"Go on!" Helga growled. "Eat some dirt!"

"I don't really like dirt," I protested. "I, uh, I prefer moldy cheese."

Susan circled her big, flat tongue around her lips. "All monsters love dirt!" she rasped.

"Eat it!" Bernard demanded.

"Eat it now!" Rachel added.

The monsters inched closer. I bit my tongue to keep from screaming.

"I — I can't eat it!" I blurted out. "Really! I can't!"

"Why not?" Rachel said. "Why can't you eat dirt?"

"Because I — uh, I'm on a diet," I said

quickly. “A special no-dirt diet. My dad will *kill* me if I break it. He’s a real monster!”

Rachel started gurgling again.

“Okay,” Bernard said in his raspy voice. “Then transform.”

“Transform? You mean, like . . . transform?” I repeated stupidly. I was stalling for time.

“Transform!” Helga shouted. “Change into your monster look!”

“What?” I gasped. *“Now?”*

“Now!” Susan screamed. “Now!”

“But the bell is about to ring,” I protested. I hoped it was, anyway. “There isn’t time.”

“Why not?” Bernard stuck his buggy eyes in my face. “I can change into my monster look in no time.”

“Well, sure, I *could* transform now,” I lied. “But my monster look is, uh, pretty extreme.”

“Monsters are *all* extreme!” Helga declared. “Do it!”

The only thing that could save me now was the bell!

Or the safety button.

But was this a *real* emergency? I wasn’t sure.

Susan suddenly dove at me.

I ducked out of the way.

Her face smashed into the Cyclone fence behind me. And she started licking the metal links.

"Hey, Bernard," Helga growled. "Remember the new kid who came last year?"

"Yeaaaaah." Bernard nodded slowly.

"Oh, him," Rachel put in. "He wasn't a monster."

"Yeaaaaah," Bernard said again. "He wasn't a monster."

The three of them stared at me.

"Really?" I managed. "Well, um, was he nice?"

Helga broke into a grin. "Nice?" she howled. "He was delicious!"

The other monsters cracked up at Helga's joke. I tried to laugh too.

What came out sounded more like a squeak.

"I'll bet you're delicious too, Liam," Bernard whispered.

Susan pulled herself away from the fence.

"Wait!" she screamed. "Don't start without me!"

The four of them pressed in even closer. I felt their hot breath on my face. I was dead meat!

"Stop!" I cried.

Helga only growled and gnashed her teeth.

Bernard flicked his tongue in and out of his mouth.

Susan licked her lips.

Rachel's drool splashed onto my sneakers.

I pulled away from the fence. Time to make a break for it!

But the monsters shoved me back again. They bared their horrible teeth.

They were about to eat me!

This was an emergency!

I ran my hand over my shirt pocket. But I couldn't feel the safety button.

Where was it?

Before I could find it, a girl burst through the circle of monsters. All I could see of her was wild brown hair.

She grabbed me by the wrist, pulling my finger away from my shirt pocket. She yanked me away from the fence.

"Back off, Marnie!" Bernard shouted. "We saw him first!"

I tried to tug my arm away. But Marnie was strong. She squeezed my wrist — hard.

"Yeah!" yelled Rachel. "Get in line, Marnie!"

"Make me!" Marnie yelled back.

With my free hand, I kept poking at my shirt pocket.

Where was that stupid button?

Marnie yanked me again. She started to pull me across the playground. I stumbled after her. The four monsters chased us.

"He's not a monster, Marnie!" Bernard yelled.

"We want him to transform," Rachel added. "But he won't."

"You mean he *can't*," growled Helga.

"Give him back, Marnie!" Susan screamed. "I forgot my lunch today!"

"Tough luck!" Marnie called back.

She pulled me over to the sidewalk. A tall, thick hedge lined the walk.

I made a leap for the hedge. But I didn't get very far. Marnie kept an iron grip on my wrist.

With my free hand, I clawed frantically at my shirt pocket. Where was that stupid button? I couldn't feel it anywhere.

Marnie tugged me down the sidewalk. For a second, I thought she was going to pull me into school.

No such luck.

Before we reached the door, she ducked through a gap in the hedge. She pulled me after her.

She was just looking for a private spot to eat me, I realized with horror.

Marnie grabbed my other wrist. Now there was no way I could reach the emergency button.

Then Bernard and his gang charged through the bushes. They surrounded Marnie and me.

"Okay, Marnie. We'll share," Rachel offered.

5

I was about to die a horrible death! Terror made my knees shake. I didn't think I could stand up much longer.

And then, to my surprise, Marnie let go of my wrists.

"No one is going to eat Liam," she announced.

"He can't transform!" Bernard yelled. "He's not a monster!"

"We want to tear off his skin," Helga growled.

"And then eat him!" Susan added, smacking her lips.

Quickly I brought my finger up to my pocket.

The button! I found it!

"I've seen him transform," Marnie declared.

You HAVE? I thought.

My finger stayed over the button. But I didn't push it.

"You have not!" Rachel sputtered.

"I have too," Marnie insisted. "But Liam only transforms under certain conditions."

"Conditions?" Bernard asked. "What conditions?"

Marnie brushed her wild brown hair away from her face. For the first time, I noticed that she didn't have bulging eyes. She wasn't drooling or licking anything. She didn't have any wood splinters sticking to her chin.

She looked . . . well, normal. Messy — but normal.

"Liam only transforms under a full moon," Marnie said.

"How do *you* know, Marnie?" Bernard demanded.

"Yeah, Marnie!" Susan growled.

"Liam just came here yesterday," Helga pointed out. "None of us ever saw him before. And you haven't, either."

"Don't be so sure," Marnie said mysteriously. "I get around. I see things. Lots of things." She turned to me. "Right, Liam?"

"Right!" I practically shouted. "Totally right!"

"I don't believe you," Rachel said. Bubbles dribbled out of the sides of her mouth. "If you've seen him transform, Marnie, then tell us. What does he transform into?"

Yeah, what? I thought. I glanced at Marnie.

But Marnie was one cool cookie. She tossed her thick brown hair and murmured, "You'll just have to see for yourselves."

"Okay!" Helga grinned. She still had big chunks of dirt stuck in her teeth. "There's a full moon tomorrow night. We'll see him transform then."

"Tomorrow night?" I pretended to be thinking about it. "Yeah, well, that could happen."

Yeah, right. I thought. And I could be elected president!

"Oh, but wait," I babbled on. "Hold it. We have that history test the next day. And, boy, I really have lots of studying —"

"Shut up!" Bernard growled. "We'll meet on the playground."

"At midnight," Rachel gurgled.

"Yesssss," Susan hissed. "At midnight. Right, Marnie?"

Marnie shrugged. "I'll be there."

They all stared at me. My heart started pounding.

"Midnight?" I croaked. "Sure. Why not?"

At last the bell rang. Bernard, Rachel, Susan, and Helga started back through the gap in the hedge.

Bernard turned to me before he went through.

"Tomorrow at midnight," he snarled. "Be here."

"Don't worry," I sneered. "I can't wait."

But inside, I was shaking.

"If you don't come, we'll find you," Bernard added. "We'll have a party and eat up your whole family!" Then he let out a horrible laugh and stomped through the hedge.

And I was alone with Marnie.

Marnie had saved me from the monsters. She even lied for me.

But, why? I didn't have a clue.

That made me nervous.

"Thanks for saving me from those . . . those other . . . uh, kids, Marnie," I stammered.

"That's okay," she said.

"Um, about tomorrow night . . ." I began.

"What about it?" she asked.

"Well, for starters," I said, "what am I going to do?"

6

Marnie only shrugged. Then, in a soft voice, she said, "I think you're like me, Liam."

Relief flooded through me. At last — someone at this stupid ghoul school who was like me! A real kid! Someone who could understand what I was going through!

I grinned. "That's the best news I've heard since I walked into Room 5 yesterday," I told her.

Marnie smiled back at me.

"Speaking of Room 5," she said, "we'd better get to class."

"Right." I followed Marnie back through the bushes. "But about tomorrow night . . . what *am* I going to do?"

"Don't worry," Marnie assured me. "We'll talk about it later."

Don't worry? Easy for her to say!

When we walked into Room 5, Ms. Barker was flicking the lights on and off.

"Quiet, class!" she called. "Settle down!"

Nobody paid any attention to her.

Bernard was chewing up his crayons. Susan stood by the wall map of the world, licking the continent of Australia.

Helga had dumped the contents of the pencil sharpener into her mouth. She was running around the room spewing pencil shavings at everybody.

Ms. Barker tried again. "Class!" she called. "It's time for your science lesson!"

But nobody listened.

Finally Ms. Barker turned to Susan. "Will you quiet everyone down, please?" she asked.

Susan peeled her tongue off Australia. She grinned and nodded at the teacher. Then she opened her mouth and let out a mirror-shattering scream. She sounded like a hundred ambulance sirens going off at once!

I clapped my hands over my ears. But I knew my eardrums would never be the same.

That scream did the trick, though. Room 5 settled down.

Ms. Barker began our science lesson by describing different poisonous plants. She told what would happen if you ate twigs from a cherry tree.

"You'll gasp for breath," Ms. Barker said. "Your heart will beat five times faster than usual. Then you'll pass out."

I never thought of eating any kind of twig. But I figured with Helga in the class, it was an important lesson.

Next, Ms. Barker told us what would happen if we ate daffodil bulbs. She ticked off on her fingers the effects: "Nausea, chills, vomiting, diarrhea . . ."

Someone poked my shoulder. I jumped. Then, slowly, I turned around.

"Here," Rachel said. She slapped a soggy piece of folded-up notebook paper into my hand.

"Thanks," I whispered.

My hands shook as I dried the note on my jeans. Was it from Bernard or Helga, reminding me about tomorrow night?

Slowly, I unfolded it. It said:

> Can you come to my house after school? Meet me by the grocery store on the corner. Nod if you can.
>
> Signed,
> Marnie

Phew! I turned around and caught Marnie's eye. I gave a nod.

My mom was right, I thought.

Having a friend at school made a *big* difference!

When school ended, I raced out the door. I didn't want any monsters to stop me. I ran down the sidewalk and out the playground gate. I rushed to the corner grocery store.

As I waited there for Marnie, I kept checking over my shoulder for Bernard and Helga. They were the monsters who scared me the most. But I didn't see them.

Marnie walked up to me a couple of minutes later.

"Hi, Liam," she called.

"Hi," I said. "Thanks for the note. Are we going to your house?"

"Actually, we're here." Marnie pointed up. "I live over the grocery store."

I followed her around to a side door. We went up two flights of wooden stairs and walked into a big kitchen.

"Wait here," Marnie told me. "I want to get something from my room. Something that might come in handy tomorrow night."

"What is it?" I asked. "A full suit of armor?"

Marnie giggled. "It's stuff you can use to fool those kids who are giving you a hard time."

She disappeared down a hallway. As I waited for her to come back, I thought how thankful I was to her. She had saved me this morning in the playground. Now she was helping me again. Without her, I might be a pile of bones lying in the playground!

Wait. What was I thinking? With Helga around, not even my *bones* would be left!

Marnie came back carrying a big box. She set it on the kitchen table and opened the lid.

"I keep all my old Halloween stuff in here," she explained. She picked up a pair of plastic vampire fangs. "These would be good for a transformation."

"Excellent!" I stuck them into my mouth and grinned.

Marnie laughed. "Not bad," she said. "Try this." She picked up a big, bulging eyeball. The iris was a muddy green. The white part was milky yellow. Red veins popped out all over it.

She handed me the eyeball. It felt cold and squishy. And the back of it was sticky. "Gross!" I exclaimed.

"Press the sticky side to your eyelid," Marnie instructed.

I did. "Hey, do I look like Bernard?"

Marnie cracked up.

The two of us spent the rest of the afternoon working on my monster outfit. We were going for a werewolf look. We cut out black fake fur and glued it to an old mask and a pair of gloves. Marnie found a shaggy black wig too.

At last I was ready to put it all on. First, I held the furry mask to my face and stretched the rubber band over my head to hold it in place. Next, I put the wig on. Then I stuck the bulging eyeball to my eyelid. I popped in the fangs. Finally, I pulled on the hairy gloves.

I checked myself out in the mirror. I looked awesome!

"Whooooo!" I howled, trying for the full monster effect.

Pretty good! But . . .

I pushed my mask up and turned to Marnie.

"Will it fool them?" I asked her.

"I hope so," she murmured. She glanced at me. "You'd better hope so too. If you don't fool them, they really will eat you alive."

7

"I *look* like a monster," I said. I checked myself in the mirror again. The bloodshot eyeball was a truly disgusting touch. "And after two days in Room 5, I know how to *act* like a monster."

"So you'll fool them." Marnie shrugged.

I peeled off the disguise. "If I could show up at the playground already wearing this stuff, I'd fool them for sure," I said. "But how can I put everything on fast enough to make it look like I'm transforming?"

"Practice," Marnie said calmly. "You'll be surprised how fast you can move when your life depends on it."

"Good point," I muttered.

"Don't worry, Liam," Marnie told me.

"When you start transforming, you'll run around, screaming and moaning. Right?"

"I guess." I hadn't really thought about this.

"Well, do it," Marnie urged. "Run to the big tree that hangs over the playground. It'll be dark under there. I'll keep Bernard and the gang busy on the other side of the playground. Then run back out and — bingo! You're a monster!"

"Bingo!" I repeated, smiling. "That sounds like a plan."

Marnie smiled. "Trust me. It's a great plan."

I thanked Marnie about a thousand times. Maybe two thousand. Then she helped me pack up my monster kit, and I hurried home.

At dinnertime, I practically inhaled my food. I had to get up to my room and start practicing my transformation.

"Liam!" Mom said. "Stop gulping your mashed potatoes! I think you're learning bad manners at that school."

I brightened. "Does that mean I can change schools?" I looked from her to my dad. "Like maybe tomorrow?"

"No," Mom snapped. "It means you should sit up and eat properly."

Finally, I finished my dinner. I dashed up to my room.

I found a pair of baggy jeans with big pockets. I put them on with a navy blue hooded sweatshirt. I stuck the eyeball in the left pocket of my jeans. The fangs went into the right pocket. I stuffed the wig, the hairy mask, and the gloves into the front pocket of the sweatshirt.

For the rest of the evening, I timed myself, taking monster props out of my pockets and slapping them onto my face and hands.

By ten o'clock, I had it down to less than seven seconds.

I hit my bed, feeling pretty proud of myself. It isn't every kid who can turn into a monster in under seven seconds!

But I didn't feel proud the next day at school.

I felt *scared*!

Bernard glared at me all morning with his big pop eyes.

Helga circled my desk, making gross chomping noises. She still had clumps of dirt between her teeth. Obviously, she wasn't big on brushing them. Or maybe she ate her toothbrush.

Rachel slimed my sneakers when I walked by her desk.

When I got up to toss something in the wastebasket, Susan came up behind me and swiped the back of my neck with her tongue.

"Stop that!" I cried.

Susan grinned. "Delicious!" she squealed, twirling around. "Maybe I won't wait until tonight!"

I staggered back to my desk. I might as well stop worrying about midnight. I wasn't sure I would live through the day!

At lunchtime, I hid in the bathroom. I was hungry. But at least when lunch period was over, I was still alive.

At recess, I begged Ms. Barker to let me stay inside. Maybe my teacher was a monster. But I had a hunch she wouldn't eat anyone in her class.

"I can clean the erasers," I offered. "Or wipe down the chalkboard. Or how about the aquarium? Maybe I could wash the fish or something."

"Go outside, Liam," Ms. Barker ordered.

I glanced at the window.

Helga was staring in at me, licking her lips.

"Please, Ms. Barker!" I begged. "They'll kill me if I go out there!"

"All right, Liam." Ms. Barker sighed. "You can stay in and help me set up for science class. We're dissecting cow eyeballs."

"No problem!" I declared.

I happily set an eyeball on each desk. Touching the slimy, icky cow eyes sure beat getting eaten alive at recess!

The class spent the afternoon cutting up cow eyes. We each made a drawing of our eye. Then Susan and Rachel volunteered to clean up. They got into a big fight and started grabbing the cut-up eyeballs and stuffing them into their mouths.

Cleanup was over in no time.

At last the end-of-school bell rang. I had made it through the day.

But could I really fool the monsters at midnight?

I glanced at Marnie. She flashed me a thumbs-up.

I smiled. I thought about how fast I could change into my monster look. I thought about my gruesome eyeball. My hairy wig.

Could I fool them? Would it work?

Nearly midnight.

I checked my gear. I had on my baggy jeans and hooded sweatshirt. I had the fangs and the eyeball in my pants pockets. I had the wig, the hairy mask, and the gloves in my sweatshirt pocket.

At the last minute, I remembered the safety button. I stuck it in the pocket with the fangs.

I checked my watch. Ten to twelve. Time to get going.

My mom and dad are sound sleepers. I knew I could sneak out of the house without waking them. But maybe I *should* wake them, I thought. To tell them good-bye!

Silently, I let myself out the back door. I headed for school under the light of the full moon. I shivered. But it wasn't from the chilly October air. I shook from fear!

As I rounded a corner by the school, I saw dark shadows in the playground. I knew it was the monsters, waiting.

Waiting for me.

I shook harder. Keep walking, I told myself.

When I got closer, I spotted Marnie in the group. Boy, was I glad to see her!

I stepped through the gate into the playground.

"Here he is!" Bernard croaked as I walked up to them. "If you're a monster, Liam, let's see you transform."

"Do it now!" Susan rasped. "Or else!" She licked her lips.

"Okay. You asked for it," I warned. "Here goes!"

8

I tilted my face up to the full moon.

I let out a shivery howl worthy of any werewolf.

Then I took off for the darkest corner of the playground.

Bernard ran after me.

"Bernard!" Marnie called. "Come back here!"

"No way!" Bernard cried. "I want to see this up close!"

I glanced over my shoulder. Bernard was right behind me. So were Helga, Susan, and Rachel! I hadn't counted on this.

I knew I could get my monster gear on in seven seconds.

But could I do it on the run?

I didn't have a choice!

I circled the playground, darting this way and that. I yowled and howled as I ran. I headed for a shadowy spot and yanked the wig out of my sweatshirt pocket.

Oh, no! There went one of my gloves.

I didn't stop to pick it up. I kept running.

I bellowed like a bull as I pulled the wig down on my head. Fake black hair hung over my eyes. And my nose. And mouth.

I had the wig on backwards!

But I kept running. I wailed and screeched.

All the while, my heart pounded like a hammer.

I was running for my life!

I slipped the furry mask out of my pocket. I smashed it onto my face. I tugged on the rubber band.

SNAP!

It broke!

How was I going to keep the mask on?

And then I knew — I *wasn't*!

Still running, I shoved the mask back into my sweatshirt pocket.

I dug my gross eyeball out of my jeans.

I slapped it onto my eyelid.

But the wig was hanging down over my eyes. The sticky stuff on the back of the eyeball didn't stick to the hair. My gruesome eyeball fell off and bounced away.

I did the only thing I could. I stuck the plastic fangs in my mouth.

Then I whirled around and faced the monsters.

Bernard, Helga, Rachel, and Susan stopped.

I clawed at the air and let out a horrible roar.

They stood perfectly still, staring at me with wide eyes.

Then Bernard said, "You must be joking."

"Plastic fangs," Helga sneered. "How pitiful."

"Want to see transforming?" Rachel gurgled. "Watch this!"

Rachel's mouth opened wide. Her arms grew long and thin. Her legs too. Hideous gray tentacles sprouted out of her ears. Giant suckers popped out all over her slimy skin.

"Gross!" I cried.

"That was nothing," Bernard scoffed. "Check this out!"

Bernard's green eyes bulged and turned orange. They glowed like two hot coals. His skin darkened to green and erupted in huge scaly warts. His skinny tongue uncoiled from his mouth like a whip. Webbed skin grew between his fingers and toes.

All the while, he kept growing. When he stopped, he was the size of a small car!

"GLOOOPH!" Bernard belched.

I turned to run. But Susan blocked my path. She stuck her tongue in my face.

"Get away from me!" I screamed.

Susan didn't budge. Her tongue grew longer and longer. It kept flowing out of her mouth. And Susan started shrinking into her tongue! Her tongue was taking over her body!

She made a sudden hissing sound and flopped to the ground. Then she slithered at my feet — a six-foot-long pink snake, covered with taste buds!

"Arrrrgh!" I cried. "Marnie! Help me!"

I glanced frantically around.

Marnie was nowhere in sight. Maybe she ran to get help.

But who could help against these monsters?

Now Helga shoved her face up close to mine. She bared her pointy teeth. Her eyes shriv-eled until they looked like raisins.

Her body hardened into a shiny brown shell. Antennas poked out of the top of her head. Leathery wings sprouted from her shoulder blades. She sprang up into the air and buzzed around my head like some oversize insect.

I shrank back against the tree. Rachel lurched toward me, walking on her tentacles. Bernard hopped closer. Susan started slithering up my legs, while Helga dive-bombed me from above.

THIS was an emergency!

I dug into my jeans pocket. My fingers made contact with the little silver button.

I pushed it — *hard*!

Nothing happened.

I punched the button again.

Still nothing.

The safety button was a total fraud! A fake!

I threw the thing at Bernard. It hit him in the eye.

"Owwww!" Bernard bellowed. Flames erupted from his jaws.

Rachel rose up on her tentacles. "Don't roast him, Bernard," she snarled. "I want to eat him raw!"

9

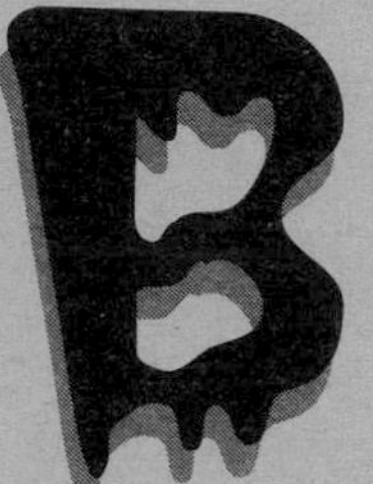

ernard lashed his tongue around my throat.

Rachel whipped a tentacle around my shoulders, pinning my arms to my sides. Susan coiled steadily up my legs.

Helga sank her pointy teeth into my ear.

I screamed in horror.

I wanted to swat her. But Rachel had a death grip on my arms.

Bernard tightened his tongue around my neck, choking off my air.

This was it. I was dead meat.

And then Susan started wailing. Louder than a siren.

I waited for my eardrums to burst.

But, wait! That scream didn't come from Susan's mouth.

It came from a police car!

The car sped through the playground gate. Other cars screeched up behind it. Their lights flashed, and their sirens blared.

Cops sprang out of the cars. They swarmed all over the playground. They shot at the monsters with huge dart guns.

Bernard was the first monster hit. His tongue pulled tighter around my neck. And then it fell away as he hit the ground with a soft, mushy thud.

Helga was next. It took four rounds of darts to bring her down.

Police rushed over to me. They unwrapped Rachel's tentacles. They pulled Susan off my legs.

"Liam!" I heard my dad cry. "Are you okay?" He ran over to me.

"I — I think so," I managed. I put a hand to my throat. Was it really over? Was I really going to live?

"But, what are you doing here, Dad?" I asked, confused. "How did you know I was here?"

"I'm not really a shopping mall cop. I'm Chief of P.U.M.S. — Police Undercover Monster Squad," Dad explained. "The safety button was really a microphone," he added. "We've been listening in on you for three days."

"You've been *what*?" I cried angrily. "You mean you *knew* what I was going through?"

My dad nodded. "I'm sorry I put you through this," he told me. "But sending you to the ghoul school was the only way we could get inside. You see, we suspected the school was overrun by monsters. But we needed proof. We couldn't make a move until the monsters transformed. Now we have that proof — thanks to you, Liam."

My dad's words rang inside my head as I walked with him over to his squad car. Wow! Thanks to me, P.U.M.S. had nabbed the monsters! The ghoul school was history! I felt great!

I glanced around the playground. Cops were everywhere. They were bagging the monsters and putting them into police vans.

Then I saw a policewoman handcuffing Marnie.

"Hey!" I cried. I ran over to her. "Stop! Untie her!"

The policewoman hesitated.

"She isn't a monster," I explained. "She's like me. She helped me against the monsters. You have to let her go."

"Sorry," the policewoman said. She quickly untied Marnie.

"Thanks, Liam." Marnie rubbed her wrists.

"Walk her home," Dad said. "The two of you had better get away from here. These monsters are still dangerous."

Marnie and I walked slowly in the moonlight, talking. When we got to the grocery store, I walked her upstairs.

"You hungry?" she asked when we reached her kitchen.

"Starving," I declared. "I was too scared to eat dinner."

Marnie brought out a bag of chocolate chip cookies. As she put them on a plate, a fly started buzzing around.

Marnie watched the fly for a moment. Then she slammed her hand down onto the table.

"Bingo!" she cried. She picked up her hand. There was the fly, squashed on her palm.

She licked it off.

"Marnie!" I cried, horrified. "But . . . what? Are *you* a monster?"

She swallowed the fly. Then she nodded.

"B-but . . . but you said you were like me!" I stammered.

"Yes, I am like you," she replied. "I'm shy."

"Huh? Shy?" I gasped.

"That's how we're alike," Marnie said. "But I just have to warn you about one thing."

"What's that?" I frowned.

Marnie leaned closer to me. She smiled as two gleaming white fangs slid down from under her upper lip.

"I bite," she said.

The Revenge

Introduction

LEFTY: I couldn't sleep last night. My dog kept barking and barking.

SLIM: So what did you do?

LEFTY: I stopped standing on its tail!

RIGHTY: Was that you or your dog I heard howling all night?

LEFTY: It was me, of course.

RIGHTY: Well, why were you howling up at the moon?

LEFTY: Because you can't howl *down* at the moon!

SLIM: Makes sense. Here's a story that's a real howl. It's called "The Revenge."

1

"Watch out!" I called frantically. "Behind you!"

My friend Isaac moved out of the way just in time. The ball I had just thrown landed in a huge mud puddle.

Fluffy jumped in after it. Mud splashed all over her.

"Whoa!" Isaac exclaimed. "Close one. Thanks, Amelia."

He bent to brush mud off his new white sneakers. He likes things clean. Isaac is the cleanest kid in the whole seventh grade.

We were hanging out on the playground after school. It had rained for two days straight. There were puddles everywhere. Including the one Fluffy was rolling around in.

I named my dog Fluffy because that's what she is. When she moves, she looks like a runaway mop.

Right now she looked like a mud ball.

I picked up her glow-in-the-dark space ball. It's supposed to bounce extra high by harnessing the power of the sun. That's what the package said, anyway. I knew it was bogus when I bought it. But I couldn't resist.

I love stuff like that. Anything weird or supernatural.

The space ball was dripping with mud. I wiped it off on my jeans. Fluffy watched me eagerly. She really loves her space ball. Whether it has the power of the sun or not.

"So where were you yesterday?" I asked Isaac. "I called your house about a million times. *Ghost Patrol* was on TV."

"I was visiting my cousin Rachel." Isaac ran one hand over his neat, wavy black hair. "Anyway, you already made me watch *Ghost Patrol* with you once, remember?"

"Oh, yeah," I muttered. "That's right."

Watching *Ghost Patrol* with Isaac was no fun at all. He kept explaining why all the weird things that happen in the movie could never happen in real life. Isaac is *not* into supernatural stuff.

I tossed the ball from hand to hand. “So how was your visit?”

Isaac wrinkled his nose. “Lame. Rachel dragged me to a fortune-teller.”

“Wow.” That didn’t sound like Isaac’s kind of thing at all. It was more up my alley. “How was it?”

“How do you think?” Isaac grumbled. “Her name is Madame Margo. She has a room above the barbershop downtown.”

He snorted. “Halfway through, she totally changed the subject. She said for a hundred bucks, she’d show us how to fly out of our bodies.”

“Huh?” I dropped Fluffy’s ball. She pounced on it.

I’ve always wished I could fly. Sometimes I have a dream. In the dream I don’t even have to think about it. I just float up into the sky and fly. It’s the greatest feeling.

“She was talking about astral projection,” Isaac said. “I’ve read about it. It’s like flying, but you leave your body behind. Madame Margo claims it’s real.”

“Cool!” I exclaimed.

Isaac rolled his eyes. “Forget it, Amelia. That stuff is totally bogus.”

Maybe he was right. He usually was.

But what if he was wrong for once? What if astral projection was possible?

It would be so awesome!

Gravel crunched behind me. Then a shadow fell over us. A big shadow. I spun around.

"What do you want?" I cried. "Leave us alone! Leave us alone!"

2

Cory Calder loomed over us. He's the biggest kid in the eighth grade. And the meanest.

He has short, crinkly red hair and a big, beefy face. His eyes are the color of mud.

"Hello, Amelia," he said to me.

He reached out and yanked on my long brown ponytail. Hard.

Then he smiled an evil smile.

"What do you want, Cory?" Isaac was trying to sound brave.

"Stay out of this, I'm-Sick," Cory sneered. *I'm-Sick* is his nickname for Isaac. "This is between me and Amelia."

Cory didn't have a nickname for me. Not yet, anyway. Up until now I had been lucky.

It looked as though my luck had run out.

"What are you talking about?" I asked.

I tried to sound brave too. But it wasn't easy. I'm tall for my age, and strong. I'm not scared of any kid in my class.

But Cory is different. He's not like a normal kid at all. He's more like a monster. A really big monster that spends its time stomping on major cities.

"You turned me in, Amelia," Cory growled.

I was crouched on the ground next to Fluffy. Cory put his hands on his knees and leaned over, so he was glaring right into my face.

"You told Principal Freakman I made that false fire alarm this morning," Cory said. "Now you're going to pay."

"It wasn't me," I protested. "I thought it was a real fire drill." The teachers all acted as if it was. So did our principal, Mr. Friedman. "I didn't tell on you. Really."

Cory snorted. "It was you. You're the only one who saw me. You were coming out of the science lab right across the hall."

I remembered seeing Cory in the hall. But I didn't notice what he was doing. Whenever I see him, I usually just concentrate on getting away before he sees me!

"This should teach you not to be a squealer,

A-Squealia," Cory said. I guess that was his new nickname for me.

I tensed up. "What are you going to do?"

Cory bent over and grabbed Fluffy's space ball out of her mouth. She whined with surprise.

He held the ball above Fluffy's head. She barked and jumped. But he jerked it away at the last second. Her jaws snapped shut on thin air.

I felt my heart start to pound. "Leave her alone!" I cried. "She didn't do anything to you."

Cory ignored me. He leaned over, moving the ball up and down. He kept it just out of Fluffy's reach. Teasing her.

Finally Cory seemed to grow bored with the game. He stood up.

"Dumb dog," he muttered. "Almost as dumb as its owner."

He turned and threw the ball as hard as he could. Fluffy bounded after it.

For a second, I was relieved. Maybe Cory was done with me now.

Then I saw where the ball was headed.

It flew across the playground and bounced into the street.

State Street. The busiest street in town. Even from here I could see dozens of cars whizzing by.

And Fluffy was tearing right toward them.

"Fluffy!" I screamed. "No!"

Fluffy didn't hear me. She raced after the ball. Her glow-in-the-dark space ball.

There was a low hedge along the street. The ball bounced right over it.

Fluffy could jump it just as easily.

The cars wouldn't see her coming. Not until it was too late.

I jammed my fingers between my teeth and whistled as loudly as I could.

And Fluffy stopped. Right at the edge of the street.

A large dump truck rolled over her ball. *SQUISH*.

I couldn't speak. All I could do was watch my dog trotting back toward me. Alive. In one piece.

Isaac was glaring at Cory. "That was a jerky thing to do, Cory," he said angrily. "Even for you."

Cory grabbed Isaac by the front of his clean white T-shirt.

"Oh, yeah?" he snarled. "You think I'm a jerk, I'm-Sick?"

"Uh — no . . ." Isaac gasped. But it was too late.

Cory grabbed a big handful of mud and

dropped it down the front of Isaac's pants. Then he wiped his muddy hand on Isaac's shirt.

"Stop it!" I yelled. "Leave him alone!" I shook with anger.

I always knew Cory was mean. But I couldn't believe what he had just done.

He had almost killed my dog.

And he wasn't even sorry about it!

Cory smirked. "Catch you later," he said. He gave Isaac one last shove, then jogged away.

Isaac watched him go, rubbing his shoulder. "What a jerk," he muttered.

"No kidding." I grabbed Fluffy and hugged her. "Somebody needs to teach Cory a lesson!"

Isaac started trying to clean himself off. But it was hopeless.

"Right," he mumbled. "Somebody like Arnold Schwarzenegger, maybe. Not somebody like us. It's impossible."

Should I tell my parents what happened? Maybe they could call the police and have Cory arrested. Attempted dog murder.

But Cory already believed I was a squealer. I didn't want to prove him right.

Then I got an idea. A really wild idea.

"I don't know, Isaac," I said thoughtfully. "Maybe getting back at Cory isn't as impossible as you think."

3

I didn't tell my parents I was going to empty my savings account the next day after school. I just did it.

The bank teller handed me the cash. "One hundred dollars," she said. "Will that be all?"

I nodded at her, trying to look like the kind of twelve-year-old who made hundred-dollar withdrawals every day.

"Thank you," I said in my most mature voice. Then I jammed the money in my pocket and scurried for the door.

I hoped she didn't call my parents. My grandmother had started the account for my birthday. And I had just withdrawn the entire amount.

Isaac was waiting for me outside.

"I still think you're crazy," he said.

I didn't answer. He'd been telling me the same thing all day.

It took only a few minutes to walk from the bank to the barbershop. A small, hand-lettered sign pointed to a narrow stairwell. MADAME MARGO, SECOND FLOOR, it said.

"Are you coming with me?" I asked.

Isaac wrinkled his nose. "Do I have to? I still think this whole idea is ridiculous." He sighed. "But I'll come if you really want me to."

That's Isaac for you. He'll do anything I ask. But he doesn't always make it easy.

"Never mind," I told him. "Just wait here for me, okay? I'll be out in a minute." I walked upstairs.

Madame Margo's room was tiny. Candles flickered everywhere. The walls were painted red. A human skull grinned out of one corner. Was it real? I couldn't tell.

"Come in, my child," Madame Margo said in a creaky voice. She sat on a large chair behind a narrow table. "Let me tell you what you wish to know."

I tried not to stare at Madame Margo. Her bright red hair was cut very short. It made her head appear tiny compared to her body. She had to weigh at least four hundred pounds! A stained purple jogging suit stretched to cover her huge rolls of fat.

"Sit," she commanded.

I perched on a rickety chair. I was already wishing I hadn't come. Maybe Isaac was right. This whole astral-projection thing was all baloney.

Madame Margo reached across the table and took my hand. "Now," she murmured. "Your name. It is coming to me. It starts with the letter 'B.' No, 'S.' "

I shook my head. " 'A,' " I corrected her. "It's Amelia."

"Of course, of course." Madame Margo rubbed my hand. Her fingers felt cool and soft. "You are a student."

Well, that was pretty obvious. I waited to see what she would say next.

"You are very shy, Amelia," she declared. Her eyes were half-closed. "You do not have many friends. But only because you are afraid to talk to people."

I rolled my eyes. Shy? Me? What a laugh. My mom always says I'm as shy as a charging rhinoceros.

"You are worried about something," Madame Margo crooned, swaying back and forth. She stroked my hand as she rocked. It tickled and made me want to pull my hand away. But I kept still.

"Your parents," the fortune-teller went on. "You are worried about them."

She opened one eye and peeked at me. I shook my head.

Madame Margo closed the eye again. "No, it's your brother you are worried about," she murmured.

"I don't have a brother," I said. In fact, I'm an only child.

"You have no brother," Madame Margo replied smoothly. As if it had been her point all along. "Only sisters. Too many sisters. That is your problem."

I sighed. No doubt about it. Madame Margo was a big fake.

"Thank you," I said, standing up. Time to get out of here.

Madame Margo's eyes flew open. "Wait!" She held up a hand.

I waited. I couldn't help it. Her eyes held me in place. They suddenly seemed to glitter. To glow. To see through me.

"I know why you came, Amelia," Madame Margo announced.

She leaned forward.

"I can help you."

4

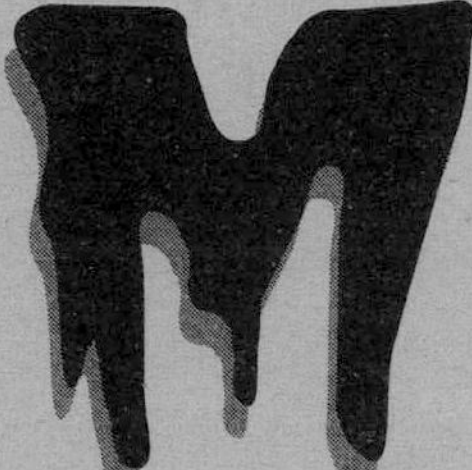

y heart started pounding. "What do you mean?" I asked.

"Sit." Madame Margo gestured at the chair.

When I was seated, she continued. "I can give you the power of astral projection as you desire. But only if you are willing to accept the danger."

I couldn't believe it — she really did know why I was there!

"D-danger?" I stammered.

The fortune-teller nodded. "The power is very dangerous," she said. "It is easy to leave your body behind. But you have only one hour in your astral form. One hour, and that is all. If you stay out longer, you will be closed out of your body. You will float aimlessly, cut off from the human world for all eternity."

I gulped. That didn't sound good.

I decided to do what Isaac would do. Ask smart questions.

"If I actually fly out of my body," I began, "does that mean I'll be invisible?"

Madame Margo nodded again. "In your astral form, you cannot be seen by human eyes."

"You said I have an hour, right?" I asked. "Do I have to use it all at once?"

"You may use it as you wish," the fortune-teller said. She waved one arm. The motion made the candles flicker. "You can make six ten-minute flights. Or three twenty-minute ones. It doesn't matter. As long as you don't go over an hour. One hour. That's all anyone gets."

I didn't know what to do. I couldn't think of any more questions. Except for one big one. *Is this for real?*

Did I really want to take a chance? Spend all my money on something that might not even be real?

I thought about Cory. It would be great to be able to get back at him. He deserved it.

Fluffy flashed into my mind. Fluffy — chasing the ball toward the busy street.

That was all it took.

I had to try. I wanted revenge.

I pulled the money out of my pocket. "I'll do it," I said.

Madame Margo smiled. Her teeth were yellow and crooked. "I knew you would."

She took the money and counted it. With a grunt, she climbed to her feet and walked around the table to stand behind me.

Suddenly my side of the room seemed very crowded. I felt her hands touch my head and tried not to flinch.

"Shut your eyes, child," she ordered.

I obeyed. This was it! Would it work?

Madame Margo started to chant. I couldn't quite catch any of the words. I wasn't even sure they were English.

After a few minutes the chanting stopped.

I opened my eyes.

The room looked the same. I felt the same.

"Is that it?" I asked. "Did it work?"

Madame Margo removed her hands from my head.

"It is done," she replied. "When you wish to fly free, you will. Now go, child."

Suddenly, all sorts of other questions came to me. I couldn't believe I hadn't thought of them before. How does it work? What do I have to do? How do I get back into my body?

I turned around to ask.

Madame Margo scowled at me. "I said *go,*" she snapped.

"But —" I began.

"Shoo! Shoo! I must rest!" Putting her hands on my shoulders, she pushed me toward the door.

"But how —" I tried again.

SLAM! The door swung shut in my face.

I stood there in the hall, feeling stupid. I had just given away my entire savings account. To someone I didn't even trust.

For something that probably wasn't even real!

Isaac was waiting right where I had left him. He was watching the barber cut a boy's hair.

"So?" Isaac glanced at me. "How did it go?"

I shrugged. "I think I just wasted a hundred dollars. My parents are going to kill me when they find out."

"Amelia!" Isaac's eyes opened wide. "LOOK OUT!"

5

I gasped as something whacked me in the side. I flew forward and hit the pavement.

"Better watch where you're going, A-Squealia!"

I glanced up. There sat Cory on his bike. He ran right into me!

I lay there on the sidewalk for a second. My knee started to throb.

I rolled over and peered down. One knee of my pants was ripped to shreds. My actual knee didn't look much better. I had a huge, ragged scrape. Pieces of gravel were embedded in my skin.

"Are you okay?" Isaac gasped.

I didn't reply. I felt like crying. But I wouldn't give Cory the satisfaction. I slowly climbed to my feet.

"What is your problem?" I demanded.

"I don't like squealers," he replied. He ran his front tire over Isaac's shoes.

"Death to all white sneakers!" Cory shouted. He sped away, laughing loudly.

"My parents are *really* going to kill me when they see this," I groaned. "My mom just bought me these pants last week."

Isaac was still gazing sadly at his sneakers. "It's not fair. He gets away with everything. It's just not fair."

He was right. It wasn't fair.

My astral-projection plan was our only chance. The only way to stop Cory's reign of terror. It had to work.

It had to!

The next day at school, I kept an eye on Cory. He was doing his usual thing. Shoving kids into lockers. Stealing lunches.

Last period, I had study hall. I told the teacher I was sick. She gave me a hall pass and sent me to the nurse's office.

But I didn't go. I walked around, searching for Cory.

I spotted him in the science lab. I peered through the glass panel in the door. His class was dissecting frogs.

Perfect.

I glanced around to make sure nobody was watching me. Then I slipped into the janitor's closet across the hall. I sat down in a dark corner next to a bunch of mops and brooms.

Then I took a deep breath. "Here goes nothing," I muttered.

There was no way this was going to work. I knew that.

But . . . what if it did?

6

I still don't know how it happened. One second I was sitting on the floor in the janitor's closet.

The next second I was gazing down at myself from the air above my own body!

"Whoa!" I cried. I couldn't say anything else for a second. I couldn't even think anything else.

I thought I was ready. I spent my whole life waiting for something like this!

But I wasn't ready. I was totally freaked out.

It took me a few minutes to calm down.

First things first. I remembered what Madame Margo had said about the one-hour time limit.

I held up my wrist to check my watch.

Then I stared at my hand.

Wow! I could see right through it. Like the ghosts in *Ghost Patrol*. There, but not there.

Madame Margo had told me I would be invisible. Could everybody see my ghostly form? Or just me?

I felt weightless. I *was* weightless. As soon as I thought about floating higher, I did. I went all the way to the ceiling.

Actually, I went *through* the ceiling.

I thought I was going to bump my head. Instead, I found myself staring at a bunch of feet. And desk legs.

I had floated up to a classroom on the second floor!

My heart thudded. Nobody seemed to see my head sticking up in the middle of their classroom floor.

Then I spotted a familiar pair of sneakers. White. With wide black tire marks across the toes.

Isaac!

I floated up and waved my hand in front of his face.

He stared at his paper. He didn't react at all.

I floated down. My legs disappeared through the floor.

I reached out my hand. And grabbed Isaac's ankle.

“Aaaaaaaaaaah!” he screamed.

Kids cried out. Isaac ducked down and peered under his desk.

He was staring right at me. But he didn’t even realize it. I clapped a hand over my mouth to keep from laughing.

“What’s the matter, Isaac?” the teacher asked.

“S-something grabbed me,” Isaac sputtered. “It felt like a hand.”

The teacher narrowed her eyes.

“Don’t be silly,” she scolded. “Back to work, everyone.”

This was so awesome! What else could I do?

I thought for a second. Then I reached out again. And concentrated on moving my hand *through* Isaac’s ankle.

Just like that, I did it.

Cool!

Nobody could see me. They couldn’t feel me, either — unless I wanted them to.

Time to head back downstairs. I had work to do.

And a time limit. I couldn’t forget about that!

I floated down. Then out of the closet. I didn’t even have to open the door.

Out into the hall. I couldn't resist. I did a somersault in the air. It was even easier than doing one in the water. I zoomed up to the ceiling, then skimmed along the floor on my stomach.

It was like my dreams. Only better. Because it was real.

I glanced at my watch. Five minutes had already passed.

Time to get started.

I floated into the science lab. Cory sat near the front.

"Listen up, people," Mr. Stockwell, the teacher, called.

Before he became a teacher, Mr. Stockwell was an air force pilot. He told us he had to quit when he got in a car accident and lost one eye. Now he wears an eye patch. It makes him look pretty tough.

"Be very careful how you handle the formaldehyde," Mr. Stockwell was saying. "It can be dangerous."

"It sure smells dangerous," a kid called out.

I took a whiff. No kidding! The stuff the dead frogs were floating in smelled disgusting.

Mr. Stockwell frowned. "I mean it, people. No fooling around. Or you'll have to answer to me."

I grinned. What a setup!

I swooped over to Cory. I waited as he moved his dead frog from the dish of formaldehyde onto the table.

Then I grabbed the frog. I made it hop across the desk.

"Hey!" Cory cried out. "This one is alive!" He bonked the frog on the head.

His fist went right through my arm. Weird!

I dropped the frog. Cory tossed it back into the dish.

I waited until he turned away for a second. Then I grabbed the frog again. I flung it as hard as I could.

Right at Mr. Stockwell.

It hit the teacher square on the back of the head. Then it splatted onto his desk. What a shot!

Mr. Stockwell spun around. "Who did that?" he shouted. Then he spotted Cory's empty dish. Cory was staring at it stupidly. "Cory! What do you think you're doing?"

"Wha-what?" Cory cried. Then he spun around and glared at his classmates. "Who did that? It wasn't me."

Everyone snickered and whispered.

Cory scowled. "I didn't do anything," he insisted. "The frog wasn't dead yet. It tried to get away before!"

"Enough," Mr. Stockwell snapped, dropping the frog back in Cory's dish. "Better take this seriously, Cory. Or you'll get an F for the project. End of story."

This was so great!

Cory bent over his frog. But he kept glancing angrily from side to side.

I checked my watch. Nine minutes had passed. Plenty of time left. What else should I do? I wanted it to be something good. Something really clever and funny.

Then a picture of Fluffy flashed into my mind. Of Fluffy running into a busy road. Because of Cory.

Maybe clever and funny wasn't the way to go after all. Maybe I should just give Cory what he deserved.

Cory reached for a scalpel. I tapped him on the top of his head. He glanced up, startled.

I grabbed the frog out of the dish again. By now, I was getting used to being invisible.

With one hand, I yanked out the front of Cory's T-shirt. With the other, I stuffed the frog down the front. Then I used both hands to squish the frog against Cory's chest.

Cory leaped to his feet with a hoarse cry.

"Cory!" Mr. Stockwell's shout rattled the beakers and test tubes. "What did I just tell you?"

Cory didn't pay any attention. He was clawing at his shirt.

I started to laugh. Then I covered my mouth with my hands. I couldn't be seen. But I wasn't sure about being heard.

Everyone was staring at Cory. Laughing. Whispering.

Cory pulled his shirt up. The frog looked as if it were glued to his skin.

He yanked at one of the frog's legs, trying to peel it off. The leg came off in his hand. The rest of the flattened frog stayed put.

"Gross!" one kid exclaimed.

Mr. Stockwell grabbed Cory by the collar and dragged him out of his seat. He peeled the rest of the frog off Cory's chest and tossed it back into the dish. "I don't think you're funny at all. But maybe Mr. Friedman will. Go to the principal's office. Right now."

Cory didn't say a word. He slunk out of the room. The smell of formaldehyde followed him.

So did I.

Out in the hallway, I watched Cory wipe his gloppy hands on his shirt. There was an odd expression on his face. It took me a second to realize what it was.

It was fear.

Cory was scared!

And *I* had done it! This was even better than I'd hoped.

I followed him to the principal's office. I thought about following him inside. Listening to what Mr. Friedman had to say.

But I decided I'd better go. I didn't want anyone to find my body while I was out floating around. And I didn't want to use up my whole hour of astral projection in one shot.

I turned and floated back down the hall. I started to laugh as I replayed the whole scene in my mind.

I did it! I got back at Cory Calder.

And it felt great!

When I reached the closet door, I floated through it. And glanced at the corner.

Hey. My body!

No. Oh, no!

It wasn't there.

7

I gasped.

Where was my body? Did someone find it? Take it to the hospital or something?

I spun around in circles. I zipped through the closet door and stared wildly up and down the hall.

Where could it have gone?

How was I ever going to find it in time?

I had one hour. Only one hour. Then I was trapped.

Then I noticed something strange.

There were no brooms in the closet. No mops. No cleaning supplies. Just papers and books.

I was in the wrong closet!

This was the supply closet. Next door to the janitor's closet.

I didn't waste any time. I dove straight through the wall. I peered around in the gloom.

There was my body. Right in the corner where I'd left it.

Whew!

I stared at it for a second. It slumped there, totally lifeless. But, boy, was I glad to see it!

The next question was, how was I going to get back in? Madame Margo hadn't told me how to do that.

So I simply closed my eyes and hoped for the best.

Once again, I hardly had to think about it. As soon as I closed my eyes, I was myself again.

My arms and legs felt heavy. I felt weighed down by gravity.

But I was so relieved to be back in my own body!

I peered at my watch. I had used up fourteen minutes. That meant I still had forty-six minutes left.

Forty-six minutes to scare Cory Calder out of his wits!

* * *

After school I headed out to the playground. I was supposed to meet Isaac there. I couldn't wait to tell him what I had done.

Isaac was there waiting for me.

But he wasn't alone.

"Take that, I'm-Sick!" Cory growled.

He had a fistful of Isaac's hair. As I watched, he shoved my friend's face into a water fountain full of rotted leaves.

I rolled my eyes. Cory hadn't learned his lesson yet.

But he would. I was going to make sure of that.

Cory let Isaac go. "Time for basketball tryouts," he said. "We'll finish this later." He ran off without spotting me.

I hurried over to Isaac. "Are you okay?"

Isaac scowled. "Take a guess." He peeled a soggy leaf off his cheek. It left a dirty brown spot.

"Well, you'll feel better when you hear what I did today," I promised. And I told him the whole story.

He didn't believe me at first. But I finally convinced him — when I told him it was me who grabbed his ankle.

"Wow. This is incredible. But are you sure

it's a good idea, Amelia?" he asked. "I just don't think you should be messing with this stuff. You don't know what could happen."

I didn't have time to argue with him. I needed to get over to the basketball tryouts.

"We'll talk about it later, okay?" I said. "I've got to go. Wait here — I'll be back in a few minutes."

I ran across the playground. The tryouts were on the outdoor courts behind the gym. But first I had to make a pit stop.

I hurried into the girls' locker room in the gym. Nobody was there. Still, just to be safe, I went to the farthest bathroom stall and locked myself in.

I checked my watch. Three fifteen.

I closed my eyes.

In my astral form, I floated quickly through the gym and out the back door to the blacktop basketball court.

Cory sat in the bleachers with the other kids. The coach was talking to them.

This was almost too easy! I floated down and tied Cory's shoelaces together.

Then I waited.

A moment later, the coach clapped his hands.

"Let's go!" he shouted. "Hit the court!"

The boys all cheered and jumped to their feet. They ran toward the court.

All except Cory. He jumped up — and fell flat on his face.

I clasped my hands over my head and shook them. Victory!

The coach gazed down at Cory. "Are you a natural klutz, Cory?" he asked. "Or do you work at it?"

Cory sat up and spit out a piece of gravel. His face was as red as his hair. He mumbled something I didn't catch.

He reached down to untie his laces. Then he jumped to his feet and jogged toward the court with the others.

I let him go. But not for long.

Every time he had the ball, I knocked it out of his hands. All his foul shots flew up over the backboard. Each pass ended up in the hands of the other team.

He couldn't even dribble in a straight line.

Thanks to me!

Finally the coach called Cory aside.

"I'm sorry," he said. "This just doesn't seem to be your sport. You'd better try something else. Maybe bowling."

"But, Coach —" Cory whined.

"I'm sorry," the coach repeated. "Get some

practice. Maybe you'll make the JV team next year — if you really work at it."

Cory's face was flaming. He gave the rest of the team a furious glance.

Then he stomped away.

I floated along behind him. This was working perfectly! And it was fun too. I could spend all day embarrassing Cory.

Oops. That reminded me. The time limit!

I'd forgotten all about it. I had no idea how long I'd been in my astral form. But it felt like a while.

I glanced at my watch.

It read three fifteen.

Three fifteen?

Whoa! Wait a minute!

That's what it had read when I started!

I stared at my watch in horror.

The second head wasn't moving.

It had stopped at three fifteen.

8

In a panic, I zoomed back toward the gym.

How long had I been out there? I had no idea. No idea!

I didn't bother with the gym doors. I zoomed right through the outside brick wall. Into the bathroom stall.

I squeezed my eyes shut and dove at my body.

A moment later, I sat up and stretched. I felt the familiar weight of my arms as I raised them over my head.

I was back. *Phew!*

But how close had I come to disaster?

I went out and glanced at the big clock on the locker room wall. Wow! I had only ten minutes left of my hour.

That was too close.

But I decided it was worth it. I'd made Cory miserable. Just the way he always made other kids miserable. Revenge was sweet.

I hurried out of the gym. Isaac was still waiting for me on the playground. I raced over to him.

"Guess what?" I cried breathlessly.

"Don't look now." Isaac stared over my shoulder. "Here comes trouble."

I glanced back. Cory was lumbering toward us.

But he didn't even bother to stop. He just shuffled past us without lifting his head.

Isaac's jaw dropped. "I don't believe it," he muttered. "He walked right past without hitting me!"

"I guess he finally learned his lesson." I turned to watch Cory walk away.

But he had come up behind me.

"I just realized," he said with a menacing grin. "There's something I forgot to do here."

He grabbed Isaac by the shoulder with one hand. The other hand balled into a fist. "Ready, aim, fire!" he cried.

He punched Isaac in the stomach.

Isaac doubled over, groaning.

"There," Cory said. "Much better." He stomped away.

I scowled after him. He still hadn't learned.

And I had only ten minutes left to teach him.

The next night I decided it was time to act.

I had a great plan. In my astral form I was kind of like a ghost. So now I was going to *act* like one.

I was going to haunt Cory.

I waited until my parents were asleep. Then I sneaked downstairs. I eased open the front door.

I heard a noise from somewhere in the house.

I held my breath. Had my parents awakened?

I didn't hear anything else. So I made my escape.

I ran all the way to Cory's house. It was almost midnight. The neighborhood was dark and quiet.

I felt nervous being out so late. It would have been safer to leave my body at home.

But I didn't want to risk it. Floating was fast, but my house was several blocks from Cory's. I had only ten minutes left. A few seconds could make a big difference.

I held my watch to my ear to make sure it was ticking.

It was. So far, so good.

I sat down on the grass and leaned back against the side of Cory's house. I hope nobody sees my body here while I'm floating, I thought. But it's late. Who would be out at this hour?

I closed my eyes.

But before I could float out of my body, something hot and wet wrapped around my wrist.

9

I gasped. My eyes flew open.

"Fluffy!" I whispered.

My dog peered up at me. Then she licked me again.

I let my breath out in a long *WHOOSH*. "Bad dog!" I scolded. "You followed me, didn't you?"

I didn't want to go all the way home again with Fluffy. But I also didn't want her to wander off while I was in my astral form. She might bark and wake someone up.

Someone who might see my body here on the grass.

"Here, girl." I patted my lap.

Fluffy jumped onto my crossed legs and sat down. I wrapped my arms around her. She licked my face.

"Stay right here," I ordered her, tightening my grip. "No wriggling."

I wouldn't be gone long. Less than ten minutes.

I closed my eyes. Soon I was gazing down at myself. Fluffy was still on my lap, sitting quietly.

It didn't take me long to find Cory's room. It was on the second floor. Through the window, I could see him sound asleep in his bed.

The window was closed. But that didn't stop me. I floated in and hovered over his sleeping body.

I had it all figured out. I was going to make him think his room was haunted.

I started by moaning like a ghost. "Whoooo!" I cried, keeping my voice low. I didn't want to wake the rest of the family.

He didn't move.

"Whooooooo!" I said, a little louder. "Aaaaaaah!"

Still nothing.

I realized I had never found out whether people could hear me or not. The answer seemed to be *not*. Too bad.

But I wasn't worried. I had more tricks up my invisible sleeve.

Across from Cory's bed, some shelves were

built into the wall. One of them held a set of encyclopedias.

I grabbed *Volume M* in one hand and *Volume R* in the other.

First I floated across the room, waving the thick books in the air. The covers flopped back and forth. The pages riffled.

Wake up, Cory, I thought. Wake up and see the floating books.

He didn't.

Maybe he needed help. I threw *Volume R* across the room.

It hit the floor. *WHUMP!*

Cory still didn't wake up.

I threw a few more things. *Volume M*. An old football. A model airplane.

Nothing.

Talk about a sound sleeper!

The seconds were ticking past.

I grabbed a whole pile of encyclopedias. Then I floated over and dumped them on Cory's sleeping body.

One hit him right on the chin. He didn't even move!

"Enough is enough!" I muttered. I grabbed him by the shoulders and shook him.

"Wake up! Wake up!" I cried. I pinched him. I pulled his hair. I slapped his cheeks.

I could see him breathing. His chest moved up and down. But his eyes remained closed.

I backed away, staring down at Cory. This was creepy.

Then I felt something on my arm. And this time it wasn't Fluffy.

It was a hand. A human hand.

I spun around.

"Hello, A-Squealia," Cory said with his evil grin.

10

I gasped in horror.

Cory floated in front of me.

I could still see his body lying there in bed.

He was an astral spirit too!

"Surprise," he taunted. "Glad to see me, A-Squealia?"

"Wha-wha —" I couldn't get the words out.

"My aunt Margo told me what you were up to," Cory said.

I gulped. "*Aunt* Margo?"

Cory nodded. "You're not the only one who can do this astral-projection stuff. She gave me the power too. As soon as I told her about what had happened to me yesterday."

He squeezed my arm tighter. "I just wish

she'd told me about this sooner. Just think of all the fun I've been missing!"

He grabbed my other arm. I couldn't move.

"Now it's my turn to teach you a lesson," he whispered.

"What do you mean?" I cried.

What *could* he do to me?

He couldn't hurt me — could he? Not as long as we were in our astral forms. I didn't have a body to be hurt!

Why didn't that make me feel safer?

"You spent a lot of time making me look stupid yesterday," Cory told me. "I figure your time must be almost up. One hour. That's all you get. I'm sure Aunt Margo told you that."

I was starting to guess what he was driving at. But I couldn't believe it.

Even Cory wouldn't be that mean.

Would he?

Cory's grip tightened. "I'm going to hold you here until it's too late. Until you're trapped this way — forever."

"No!" I cried. "You can't! Please! Let me go."

I tried to wrench my arms free. But he was too strong.

Then I concentrated on floating through

him. I pictured my arms slipping through his grasp like smoke.

But I couldn't break free. Cory's hands gripped me tighter.

"Let me go!" I demanded. I kicked him in the shin as hard as I could.

He just laughed. Then he stepped on both of my shoes with one of his big, bare feet.

I was trapped!

I remembered seeing a clock on Cory's bed-side table. I twisted my head around. How much time did I have?

"No," I gasped. "No!"

I had one minute left.

One minute. And then I would be shut out of my body.

Forever.

11

"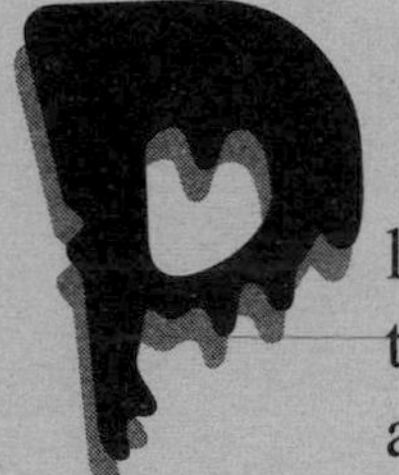lease, Cory!" I begged. "I'll do anything! I'll do all your homework for a year. I'll be your slave for life. Just let me go!"

Cory didn't even answer. He just grinned and held on.

He wasn't going to let me go.

Cold despair welled up inside me. I started struggling again. But I knew it wouldn't do any good.

Cory knew it too. He held on tight. And stared at me.

Suddenly his expression changed. "Ouch!" he cried out.

For a second, I was too startled to notice he had let go of my arms. But then I realized he had.

I shoved him backwards. With one jump I was out of his reach.

But he wasn't even paying attention to me. He was busy. Yelping with pain. Hopping up and down from foot to foot.

And now I could see why. There was something jumping around behind him.

A third astral form.

"Fluffy!" I cried.

I had been holding the dog when I floated out of my body.

She must have floated up with me!

Fluffy growled at Cory. She snapped at him again, and he jumped away.

I shot a glance at the clock. Thirty seconds left. I had to get back to my body. Now!

I darted to the window.

"Hey!" Cory floated over to block my way.

Too late.

I grabbed Fluffy — and leaped out the window.

I floated down . . . down . . . I could see my body below.

Would I make it in time?

I closed my eyes.

For a second, I couldn't tell. Was it happening? Was I returning to my human form?

I felt my limbs grow heavy. I opened my eyes.

I was back!

I jumped to my feet.

"That was close, wasn't it, Fluffy?" I cried.

But there was no answering bark.

"Fluffy?" I stared around. "Fluffy?"

Where was she?

Had she panicked when her astral form returned? Had she run away in terror?

I called her again. But, still, she didn't appear. I hoped she was on her way home.

I heard a door slam nearby. Cory came tearing around the side of the house. This time he was totally real and solid. He was still wearing his pajamas.

"You can't get away from me, A-Squealia!" he yelled. "I'm going to have my revenge!"

I turned to run. But it was too late. Cory grabbed my arm.

"Which do you like better?" he sneered. "Your stomach or your nose?"

I shut my eyes, preparing to be punched.

But Cory dropped my arm. "Hey!" he yelled. He howled with pain and grabbed his bare ankle.

I watched him dance around in the middle of his yard. First he yanked one leg up. Then he flailed his arms. Then he raced around in circles, hopping up and down.

Finally he ran back into the house. His front door slammed shut. And the night was quiet again.

"Fluffy?" I murmured. "Did you do that? Where are you?"

She was nowhere to be seen. But then I felt her lick my hand.

"Fluffy!" I knelt on the lawn. She leaped into my arms. My dog! I could feel her!

But I couldn't see her.

"Oh, no!" I exclaimed. How could this have happened?

Fluffy was still in astral form!

I ran from yard to yard. I searched the whole neighborhood. But I couldn't find her little mop of a body anywhere.

After an hour had passed, I knew it was too late. I wasn't ever going to find it.

I hugged my dog's invisible body. Her invisible tongue licked my cheek.

"Poor Fluffy," I whispered, holding her tight. "It's all my fault. I got you into this. I'm sorry. I'm so sorry!"

I'm still sorry about Fluffy. But things could be worse.

Fluffy doesn't seem to mind being stuck in her astral form. It's easier for her to sneak up on cats now. She even caught a bird last week. She let it go without hurting it. But I bet it's still wondering what happened.

Having an astral dog is actually pretty cool. I take her with me everywhere I go. Even to school. The teachers don't mind.

They don't even know. They can't see her.

And the best part? Isaac and I don't have to worry about Cory anymore.

Fluffy keeps him in line.

The Mummy with My Face

Introduction

SLIM: Our next story is about two kids who get lost in an ancient Egyptian pyramid.

RIGHTY: I got lost in an ancient Egyptian pyramid once.

SLIM: What did you do?

RIGHTY: I called for my mummy!

LEFTY: Yuck. That joke is so old, it has mold growing on it!

RIGHTY: Don't mention mold. I found a loaf of bread in the kitchen that was so old, it was covered with thick green mold.

LEFTY: What did you do?

RIGHTY: I ate it fast so I wouldn't have to share it with you two!

SLIM: Right now, I'd like to share our story with our readers. It's called "The Mummy with My Face." About halfway through, the mummies come alive!

LEFTY: We wouldn't have a story if they didn't!

1

"The ancient Egyptians built their pyramids from huge blocks of limestone," the tour guide declared. "You're probably wondering where they got that limestone."

Ha! Not me. The *last* thing I wondered about was where the Egyptians got their limestone.

I wanted to hear about the mummies.

My name is Norm Parker. I'm eleven. My parents came to a teaching convention in Cairo, Egypt, and they brought my sister, Claire, and me with them. Mom and Dad had to go to meetings today, so they sent us on a tour of the pyramids.

Claire is twelve, and she loves all this ancient Egyptian stuff. It's not exactly my favorite subject. But I figured the mummies would be exciting, right?

Wrong.

The guide hadn't even *said* the word "mummy" yet. All he talked about was sand and silt and limestone.

Our tour group walked toward the Great Pyramid of Khufu. "Most of the limestone came from nearby quarries," the guide continued. "But sometimes the Egyptians went clear across the Nile River to get it."

I yawned.

"Norm!" Claire poked me in the side. "Pay attention." She is always poking me. She thinks an older sister has the right to poke people younger than she is.

"I can't pay attention," I complained. "This is *so* boring!"

Now the guide was talking about copper chisels.

"Don't tell me you think this is interesting," I whispered to Claire.

"It is," she insisted. "If you'd stop complaining and listen, you might learn something." Claire is a good sister. But sometimes she's about as much fun as a stomachache.

"The Egyptians were among the first people to use stone for their buildings," the guide told us.

"Oh, wow!" I muttered. "Wait until I tell all my friends about that!"

The couple next to us scowled at me. "Shh!" the man whispered. "Some of us would like to hear about this."

"Sorry," Claire said quickly. She shot me a dirty look.

I sighed. If only I were back at the hotel. I could swim and order room service and play computer games. But Mom and Dad wouldn't be finished with their meetings for four more hours.

I was stuck.

Unless . . .

I reached into the pocket of my shorts and pulled out Dad's cell phone.

"What are you doing?" Claire demanded.

"I'm going to call Mom and Dad and ask them to come get us." I flipped the phone open. "Make that *beg* them."

Claire scowled at me. "I don't want to leave. Besides, Dad said only to call in an emergency."

"This *is* an emergency!" I whispered. "I'm dying of boredom!"

I checked the list of numbers Dad had given me and started calling. Mom and Dad weren't at the first number anymore. A woman at the second number said they had gone to lunch. She didn't know where.

I closed the phone and stuffed it back into my pocket. So much for getting rescued.

"Come on, Norm." Claire pointed to the tour group. They were way ahead of us. "We have to catch up."

"Okay, okay," I grumbled. I began walking. *Slowly*.

Claire glared at me. "Will you hurry up?"

"Wait a sec. I have an idea. Why don't you go on without me?" I suggested. "I'll just walk around by myself and meet up with you later."

Claire's mouth dropped open. "You can't do that!"

"Why not?"

"Because . . . because it's not allowed," she replied.

I rolled my eyes. Couldn't she forget about being the big sister just *once*?

Claire squinted down the path again. "Oh, no! I can't even see the group anymore!"

"Good riddance," I muttered.

Claire grabbed my arm and started to pull me along with her. "If we lose the tour group, it will be *your* fault. Now, come on!"

"Excuse me," a deep voice said.

We turned around.

A tall, dark-haired man stood in front of us. He had a short black beard and wore a long white robe.

Where did he come from? I wondered.

"See?" Claire whispered to me. "We're in trouble already."

"I know we got behind," I said to the man. "But I just want to walk around by myself. I promise not to bother anybody. So please don't make me go back to the tour group, okay? I don't mean to be rude, but I am soooo bored!"

"Yes, I couldn't help overhearing you," the man replied. He raised his eyebrows. "You were looking for adventure. Instead, you got a lecture."

"Yeah." I pointed to Claire. "My sister likes it, but not me."

"Allow me to introduce myself. My name is Ari. And don't worry, I won't send you back to the tour," he told me with a smile. His teeth gleamed.

"As for adventure," he added, "perhaps I can help."

2

"Adventure? Yes!" I pumped my fist. "That's just what I was looking for."

Claire rolled her eyes. "*I* was already having a good time."

"Come with me. I will take you into a pyramid that has not been opened to the public yet," Ari told us. "Just think — you'll be the very first tourists to enter it."

"Really?" I cried. "Are you with the tour? Are you a tour guide?"

He nodded. "I believe in a different type of tour."

I smiled at Ari. "No lectures about limestone, right?"

"No lectures, I promise." Ari's eyes glittered. He burst out laughing. "Definitely no lectures!"

What's the joke? I wondered. What I said wasn't *that* funny.

"Okay, let's go," Claire said.

Still chuckling, Ari turned. He led us down the path in the opposite direction from the tour group.

"So how old is this pyramid?" Claire asked. "What pharaoh was it built for?"

"Not a pharaoh," Ari replied. "It was built for a wealthy Egyptian family. Legend has it that they were also evil sorcerers. And because of their evil, a curse was put on them."

I whistled. "What kind of curse?"

"A horrible curse." Ari lowered his voice. "When they died, they were not allowed passage to the afterlife. So their souls are trapped with their bodies inside the pyramid — forever."

"Creepy," I declared. "So this pyramid is supposed to be haunted?"

Claire snorted. "It's just a *legend,* remember?" She turned to Ari. "My little brother believes everything you tell him."

I wanted to shove her face in the sand. But there wasn't time. Ari walked very quickly. I had to jog to keep up.

"Yes. It is a legend," Ari continued, his dark eyes flashing. "But a very powerful one. You see, before the last member of the family died, he swore eternal revenge."

"On who?" I asked.

Ari narrowed his eyes at me. "On the living, of course," he replied seriously. "On you and me and your sister. On anyone who dares to enter their pyramid."

He stared at me for a long while.

This guy is weird, I thought. But I felt a shiver of fear. Did he really believe in this curse?

"Ah!" Ari turned down another path and stopped, pointing. "There it is!"

The pyramid stood alone, far away from everything else. The wind had blown mounds of sand against its base. A lot of the ancient stones were cracked and crumbling.

Behind it, the sand stretched away for miles and miles. I couldn't see the tour group anymore. I couldn't hear them, either. I couldn't hear anything but the sound of the hot wind.

I glanced around.

No guards. No workers. Nobody but us.

Ari led us to the entrance. He motioned for us to follow him in. "Good luck," he whispered.

3

I peered inside. I couldn't see a thing in front of me. Just endless blackness. I felt a flicker of fear. Another shiver.

"It's awfully dark in there," I murmured.

"Indeed it is," Ari agreed. "And it will get even darker once we go down into the chambers."

Pitch-dark rooms, way under the ground? Where evil sorcerers were buried?

Okay, so it was just a story. I couldn't help it. I felt really frightened.

But I couldn't say a word. If I wimped out now, Claire would never let me forget it.

I grabbed my sister's arm. "Uh . . . if you're afraid, we don't have to do this," I whispered to her.

Ari loomed over us. "Is there a problem?"

"No — no problem," I stammered. "No problem at all. Let's go."

Oh, well, at least I won't be bored anymore, I told myself.

"Excellent," Ari declared. "Now remember to stick close together. As I said, it will be very dark. And many parts of the tomb are still unexplored. Since I have the only flashlight, we don't want to get separated."

Separated? I shivered again.

Ari stepped inside and started down a dark passageway.

Claire and I followed behind him. Our footsteps echoed off the stone floor. Dust drifted through the air. I sneezed. The sound seemed to echo for miles.

The passage grew narrower and narrower. We had to walk single file. Claire walked behind Ari. I stayed close behind her.

The passageway began to slope down. The air grew cold and wet.

"We are heading underground now," Ari called out. His voice sounded far away. His light bounced off the ancient stone walls. His white robe appeared to float ahead of us in the thick darkness.

Like a ghost, I thought.

The passage twisted to the right, then to the left. The slope grew steeper. I had to dig my heels in to keep from bumping into Claire.

"How deep underground does this tunnel go, Ari?" Claire called out. She always has to get the facts.

"No one knows — yet!" he replied. "Perhaps you will be the first."

The passage twisted to the right again. It grew so narrow, my shoulders brushed against the walls. The ceiling was lower too. We had to bend over to keep from scraping our heads. I could feel dust sifting into my brain.

"Amazing, isn't it?" Ari called out. His voice sounded muffled, far away. And I couldn't see the glow of his white robe anymore.

"Slow down!" I called.

"Don't worry. I'm not far ahead of you," he shouted back.

I don't like this, I thought. Why is Ari going so fast? And if he is a tour guide, why didn't he have flashlights for Claire and me?

Claire suddenly stumbled. I crashed into her and scraped my elbow on the rough stone. "Ow!"

"Are you okay?"

"Yeah. Keep going," I urged her. "I don't

want to get separated from Ari. What's his rush, anyway?"

"I don't know." Claire hunched over and hurried along the passage as fast as she could. "Hey, Norm? Do you realize we're actually in a tomb? With people who died thousands of years ago?"

"Thanks for reminding me."

"Ha. You're scared." Claire giggled. "What's the matter? I thought you wanted to see some mummies."

Not anymore, I thought. I wanted to see daylight and blue sky. This place was creeping me out.

After a couple of minutes, the passage stopped sloping down. And my head didn't scrape the ceiling anymore. "It's about time," I muttered. "I can finally stand up straight."

"You can hold your arms out too," Claire told me. "Try it. I think we're in a room or something."

I stretched my arms out. I didn't feel a thing. Just air.

I walked a few steps. No walls touched me. No ceiling above my head.

"Hey, Ari?" I called out. "Where are we?"

No reply.

I glanced around.

No flickering flashlight. No ghostly white robe in the darkness.

"Ari?" I called again. "Ari!"

Silence.

Ari was gone.

4

"Ari, where are you?" Claire and I both called. "Ari?"

Still no answer.

"Norm?" Claire huddled close to me in the darkness. "What's going on? Why doesn't he answer?"

"I — I don't know," I stammered.

Claire and I shouted his name over and over. The sound of our voices bounced off the stone walls and echoed around us. When it stopped, we held our breath and listened.

Silence.

"How could he just disappear like that?" Claire cried. "It's impossible."

"Yeah," I agreed. "Unless . . ." My heart began to hammer.

"What?"

I swallowed nervously. "Unless he disappeared on purpose."

Claire gasped. "But why would he do that?"

"I don't know." My hands felt clammy. "Remember how he grinned when he told us about the legend? Maybe the joke is on us."

"What do you mean?"

"Maybe Ari isn't a tour guide. Maybe he led us into some kind of trap," I murmured. "I — I never wanted to do this. I tried to get you to say no."

"Liar!" Claire cried. "I didn't want to come down here. I wanted to stay with the group. You're the one who was so excited about following him into this stupid pyramid."

I started to reply. But Claire gasped. "Norm, look! There's a light!"

I turned and spotted a pale yellow light flickering in the distance. "Ari?" I shouted.

No answer.

"Come on!" I took Claire's hand and pulled her through the darkness.

As we drew closer to the light, I realized what it was. A burning torch, set in the wall of the chamber. Did Ari put it there?

Who cares? I thought. At least we'll be able to find the tunnel and get out of here. I took the torch down and swept it around the room.

The place was huge and completely empty. Just a bare floor and flaking stone walls.

And each wall had at least two low openings cut into the thick stone, leading into dark tunnels.

"Norm?" Claire's voice quivered. "Which tunnel did we come through?"

"I . . . I can't remember." My hand shook. The torch wavered back and forth, casting weird shadows on the walls. My knees felt wobbly. I was suddenly so scared, I couldn't move.

If we picked the wrong tunnel, we might never get out.

We would wander through the ancient pyramid tunnels forever, like rats in a maze.

And no one would come looking for us.

Because no one knew we were here.

Don't panic, I told myself. Not yet.

"Let's pick a tunnel and go just a little way into it," I suggested. "If it feels wrong, we'll try another one."

Sticking close together, Claire and I crossed the empty chamber and ducked through one of the low openings. I held the torch high and peered inside.

Another chamber. Smaller than the other one. And not empty.

A box stood against the far wall, covered with dust and cobwebs. A long, low, wooden box, shaped like a coffin.

A mummy case.

My knees felt like jelly as I remembered what Ari had said. This pyramid had been built for a family of sorcerers.

An evil, cursed family.

Out for revenge — on the living.

I squeezed Claire's hand. "Let's get out of here."

We started to move, but a sound made us both stop.

A creaking sound, like an old wooden door.

I held the torch higher.

And froze in terror.

Creaking and whining, the lid to the mummy case slowly, slowly swung open.

5

I tried to scream — but no sound came out.

Claire and I turned to run and crashed into each other.

Our feet got tangled up, and we both stumbled to the floor. The torch flew from my hands and rolled across the room.

I knew I had to get it. If it went out, we'd be stuck in the pitch dark again. "Get off me, Claire!"

"What do you think I'm *trying* to do?"

I finally got my legs free and scrambled across the floor. I snatched up the torch and held it high.

The lid to the mummy case stood open. Dust and broken cobwebs drifted through the air around it.

Nothing else moved.

Claire grabbed my arm. "What's going on?" she whispered. "Why did it open? Is there a mummy in there?"

"Only one way to find out," I replied, trying to sound brave. Claire always acts as if she's a grownup and I'm a baby. But she was shaking like a frightened baby now.

We crept closer to the painted wooden case. I held the torch higher and peered in.

A slender, cloth-wrapped shape smeared with tar lay in the bottom of the case. Still. Silent.

"It's not very big," Claire observed in a hushed voice.

"People were smaller back then," I pointed out. "Or maybe it was a kid."

Staring into the flickering torchlight, we gazed down at the little mummy for a long time. It was hard to believe it had once been a living, breathing human being.

"Come on, let's try one of the other tunnels," I said finally.

For once, Claire didn't argue with me. "Yes. Let's go," she agreed.

As we turned to go, something on the wall above the mummy case caught my eye. I held the torch higher.

Carved into the stone wall were ancient Egyptian letters and drawings. And then, in English, the words: TOMB OF PRINCE KHOTEP-DUR.

The torchlight fell over a framed picture. An image of somebody's face.

I held the torch close and peered at it.

The picture showed a boy with brown eyes, and dark curly hair that flopped onto his forehead. His face was skinny, and his ears stuck out. He had a dimple on the right side of his mouth.

My heartbeat pounded in my ears.

"Oh, no!" I gasped. "It can't be!"

6

"What is it?" Claire cried.

"Look at the picture!"

Claire leaned closer. She stared at the image. Then she stared at me.

"Norm — it's *you*!" she gasped.

I nodded, unable to speak.

"It's your face," Claire whispered. "Your eyes, your ears. Your dumb crooked smile — everything!"

"I know," I choked out. I couldn't take my eyes off the picture.

How did it get here? What was a picture of me doing over a mummy case?

Claire poked me in the side. "Come on. Let's get out of here and try another tunnel."

"Okay," I said, unable to take my eyes off the picture. "Can't you stop poking me for once?"

She didn't reply. We both heard another creaking sound.

I froze again. My skin prickled.

Slowly, I glanced over my shoulder.

A hand reached up from the mummy case.

A bony hand with black, clawlike fingernails.

"The mummy!" Claire screamed. "It's alive!"

I wanted to scream. I wanted to run. But all I could do was stare in terror.

The mummy's hand rose higher. Its hideous nails clawed at the air. An arm appeared. Strips of decayed cloth hung from its rotted tar.

Slowly, the mummy's head rose up over the coffin side. More strips of rotting cloth hung from its face. The tar oozed from its eyes and down its head.

Slowly, it turned to face us. Its neck creaked like a rusty hinge. Its cracked, tar-covered lips peeled back in a snarl.

My legs finally unfroze. "Run!" I shouted.

We bolted for the door.

A deep, rumbling noise echoed through the room.

I skidded to a stop, staring in horror. Two thick slabs of stone slid across the entrance. They slammed together with a thundering boom. A cloud of dust filled the air.

I dropped the torch, raced to the doorway, and tried to pry the slabs apart.

They wouldn't budge.

"Norm!" Claire screamed.

I spun around.

The mummy was out of the coffin, hunched on its feet.

Strips of cloth dangled from its horrible, twisted arms and legs.

Its black-tarred face glistened in the torch-light. Its eyes were sewn shut, so that it appeared to be asleep.

But it wasn't sleeping.

It raised its arms, holding its clawlike hands out.

Then it began to stagger toward us.

Panting in terror, Claire and I dug our fingers between the stone slabs and pulled.

The stones didn't move an inch.

"Pull!" I yelled. "Harder!"

We pulled again.

The stones didn't move.

But the mummy did. It lurched steadily toward us, grunting with each staggering step.

7

I pressed my back against the stone door.

The mummy was halfway across the room now, shuffling toward us.

"Keep trying the doors!" Claire screamed. She dug her fingers in between them. "Norm, keep pulling!"

"It won't work!" I cried. "They weigh a ton. We can't move them!"

With its head down, the mummy staggered another step. As it moved, its legs cracked and split with a horrible ripping sound. Its blackened face loomed closer. Its hideous nails clawed at the air.

Reaching for *me*.

I grabbed Claire's hand and pulled her along the wall.

The mummy stopped. Lifted its head. It seemed to be listening. Or maybe sniffing the air.

Hunting.

Then it turned and began staggering in our direction.

We slid farther along the wall.

The mummy turned again.

My teeth started to chatter. I kept thinking about that portrait of me on the tomb wall.

Why was it there? Why was the mummy chasing after me now?

Claire stumbled and fell to the floor. I grabbed her arm. "Get up! Hurry!"

"I'm trying!" She pulled herself to her knees.

The mummy staggered closer, grunting and groaning.

I hauled Claire up and scrambled a couple of feet along the wall. My hand banged up against something hard.

A stone lever, jutting out from the wall!

Maybe this will open the door, I hoped.

I didn't hesitate. I pushed down on it.

Yes! It moved — but only an inch.

"Help me!" I cried to Claire. "On three, push down as hard as you can! One!"

The mummy staggered closer.

No time. No time. No time.

"Two!"

Closer.

"Three!"

We slammed the stone lever down.

A deep rumbling noise echoed in the chamber. "Yes!" I cried. "We did it!"

Claire and I gazed at the door.

Open. Please — open!

No.

Another rumbling sound. The door still didn't move.

"What's going on?" Claire cried frantically. "Why doesn't the door open? Where's that noise coming from?"

"I don't know! I can't . . ." I stopped with a gasp, staring down in horror.

The floor was sliding apart! A wide crack appeared in front of our feet. Growing wider . . . wider.

We jumped back.

The mummy stood on the other side of the gap. It stretched its arms out. Its bony hand scraped my chest.

"Ohhhhhh." A moan of horror escaped my throat.

It touched me.

It *touched* me!

Claire and I jumped back again. I felt the rough stone of the wall against my back.

With a grinding roar, the floor split apart.

My toes slipped over the edge.

Claire grabbed for me.

And we started to fall.

8

"ooo!" I wailed as we dropped.

Faster. Faster.

I held my breath, waiting to plunge straight down.

But instead of falling through the air, we slid down a steep, sandy ramp.

I flailed wildly, struggling to grab on to something. But I was dropping too fast.

I slid faster and faster, until I shot through an opening and tumbled onto a flat, dusty floor.

Claire slid out behind me and bumped to a stop against my back. For a second, we just sat there, breathing hard.

Then I glanced around.

We had landed in another chamber, deep underground. Two torches flickered brightly on the walls. Thick dust hung in the air.

"At least the mummy didn't fall with us." I sighed.

"Yeah, but look at those!" Claire pointed a shaky finger across the room.

At least a dozen mummy cases lined the walls.

I jumped to my feet and squinted around again. I spotted a low opening on the far wall. Another passageway.

"Maybe that will take us out," I told Claire. "Come on. And cross your fingers."

I grabbed one of the torches, and we started across the room.

But before we reached the door, I spotted another mummy case with a picture over it. And more words carved into the wall. We stopped and stared.

TOMB OF PRINCESS AMEN-TOPEK, the sign said.

The picture showed a girl with a round face and reddish brown hair. A turned-up nose with freckles on it. A tiny mole above her upper lip.

"It's me!" Claire gasped.

I swallowed hard. "Yes," I murmured. "I don't believe it. But it's definitely you."

I rubbed my arms. The hair on them was standing straight up.

"Let's get out of here," Claire moaned. "Now!"

We started toward the passageway.

As we reached the middle of the floor, loud creaks suddenly filled the room.

We spun around.

The lids. The coffin lids. They were all sliding open.

And, grunting and groaning, the mummies were climbing out.

"No — please — no!" Claire murmured.

Trailing strips of cloth, the mummies climbed from their coffins. They staggered across the room.

Their skin cracked and split as they moved. Their clawlike fingers stretched out toward us.

We forced ourselves to spin away. We started to run.

"Nooo —!" I cried out when I saw the mummy move to block our path.

I grabbed Claire's hand, and we dodged to the left.

Another mummy lumbered into our path. Its arms stretched out. Its bony fingers clawed the air.

I staggered backwards, dragging Claire with me. We spun around.

Two more mummies stood in our way. "They're surrounding us!" Claire screamed. "We can't get to the passage!"

We whirled one way, then another.

Trapped.

Think. I forced myself to concentrate. You have to think of a way out.

Then I remembered. The cell phone!

I should have thought of it before! I could get the operator to call the Cairo Police.

But would it work this far underground?

I yanked it out of my pocket.

The mummies staggered closer.

I flipped the phone open.

The mummies stopped moving. They seemed to be watching me.

I punched 0 and held the phone to my ear.

A crackling noise came over the line.

Static.

I shook the phone and punched 0 again.

Static.

"I can't get through!" I told Claire.

"Keep trying!" she urged.

I punched 0 again. Nothing but static.

Frantic, I punched all the numbers. 1. 2. 3 . . . all the way up to 0 again!

I heard only the crackle and sizzle of static.

"It's no good!" I cried. "It's not working!" I closed the phone and slipped it back in my pocket.

The mummies had stopped. But now they began to move again.

"They're closing in on us!" Claire cried. "There's no way out."

I stared at the circle of mummies. Their tar-blackened faces loomed closer. Their eyes were shut, their mouths twisted.

What could we do?

What?

"Lie down," I told Claire.

"What?"

"Lie down and play dead." I took her arm and pulled her to the floor. "Or we'll never make it out of here alive."

9

Ari stood in a room next to the mummy chamber and stared at the television screen on the wall. The screen flickered a couple of times. Then the image became crystal clear.

There they are, Ari thought. The two young tourists, trapped inside a circle of mummies. He watched as the mummies drew closer.

Ari couldn't hear the kids' voices, but he didn't need to. He could see the terror on their faces.

The boy grabbed the girl's arm. The girl's face grew pale.

The mummies staggered closer.

The kids sank to their knees. Then they toppled facedown onto the chamber floor.

"Wonderful!" a voice declared.

Ari turned around. Dr. Martez, a chubby bald man, sat in front of a control panel full of knobs and levers. His blue eyes gleamed happily.

"Isn't it great, Ari?" Dr. Martez asked. "The kids are terrified! Look at them! Look at them screaming and backing away. Look at the horror on their faces!"

Ari nodded grimly. "Yes, sir. We have frightened them."

"Did you see the kids' faces when they recognized their pictures?" Dr. Martez cried gleefully. "Did you see the shock? The total fear?"

Ari turned back to the television screen. His eyes widened in alarm.

The two kids were still down on the floor. Not moving.

Not moving.

And the mummies had disappeared.

Ari gasped. "Dr. Martez, the mummies are gone! And I . . . I think something has happened to those kids!"

"What?" Dr. Martez leaped to his feet. "That can't be!" He squinted into the screen, and his smile faded quickly.

"Ari," he gasped. "Something terrible has happened."

10

"Look at them!" Ari shouted. He pointed to the screen. "They're not moving. And what happened to the mummies?"

"I — I don't know!" Dr. Martez reached for the control panel and jerked a lever.

"Forget that for now!" Ari cried. "We have to help those kids!" He leaped to the door and flung it open.

And gasped in surprise.

A mummy stood in the doorway.

"Dr. Martez!" Ari croaked.

The scientist's face grew white as he saw the mummy. "Impossible! How did it get here?"

"I don't know," Ari choked out. "But — it isn't alone." Ari pointed.

Behind the first mummy stood a second

one. A third. A fourth. The mummies groaned and sighed. Their sour odor filled the room.

"They're all here!" Dr. Martez gasped. "All of them!"

For a moment, no one moved.

Then the first mummy began to stagger forward. The others followed, trailing strips of decayed cloth. Their bones creaked. Their bandages ripped. Their fingers clawed the air.

Ari and Dr. Martez backed across the office, gasping in fear.

"What do they want with us?" Ari whispered. "What?"

11

"The mummies have gone completely haywire!" Dr. Martez shrieked. "This is impossible!" His eyes bulged, and he shook his head in disbelief.

The mummies kept staggering forward. Reaching for the two terrified men.

Ari glanced around in panic. "Do something!" he urged. "Try your controls."

The scientist stumbled to the panel and frantically began to turn knobs.

The mummies didn't stop.

Dr. Martez flipped a lever.

He flipped it again. And again.

The mummies still kept coming.

"The controls don't work!" Dr. Martez cried. "I can't understand it."

Dr. Martez grabbed hold of a lever. A

mummy clamped its hand around his wrist. Its other hand reached for his throat.

"Do something!" Ari shrieked again.

"I can't stop them!" Dr. Martez screamed. "I have no control! The mummies are alive. ALIVE!"

12

“Norm?” Claire whispered. “Do you hear anything?”

I held my breath and listened.

Silence.

I slowly raised my head about an inch.

Nothing in front of me.

I lifted my head higher.

Still nothing.

So far, so good.

I rose to my knees and glanced around.

The chamber was empty.

“They’re gone, Claire.” I took her arm and pulled her to her feet. “It worked. I don’t know why. But it worked.”

I tucked the cell phone back into my pocket.

Claire shook her head. She stood up and

brushed herself off. “Norm, did I ever tell you — you are a genius.”

“Never,” I replied.

“Well, I’m saying it now,” she said. “Playing dead was brilliant!”

“Yes, it was,” I replied. For once, Claire and I agreed on something!

“Where do you think they went?” Claire glanced nervously at the mummy cases. “Back to their coffins?”

“I don’t know, but let’s not stick around to find out,” I replied. “Let’s get out of here.”

We hurried toward the passageway. We almost reached it.

But then a tall, bent mummy lurched out from the shadows and blocked our way.

“Oh, no!” Claire moaned. “Another one!”

The mummy stepped forward, reaching out its hands menacingly.

We stumbled back. My heart raced.

“The cell phone! Try it again!” Claire yelled. “It’s our only hope!”

I dug into my pocket for the phone and tried to pull it out.

The antenna snagged on a thread in my pocket.

The phone was stuck!

"No!" I groaned. I yanked frantically at the phone. But it wouldn't budge.

The mummy's hands groped toward my throat.

I screamed and staggered back — into the wall.

My teeth started to chatter. The mummy wants to kill us! We'll die down here in the darkness!

I tugged harder. Harder.

I heard cloth rip in my pocket. The phone finally came loose.

I yanked it out.

The mummy's fingers scratched at my throat.

I screamed and almost dropped the phone.

With a shriek, Claire grabbed one of the mummy's arms and jerked it away from me. Rotten cloth and dried flesh fell to the floor.

I tried to flip the phone open. My fingers slipped.

The mummy's other hand swung up. Both hands circled my throat. "Get it off!" I croaked.

Claire tried to pry its fingers loose. One finger snapped off with a crack and crumbled into dust in Claire's hand.

I brought the phone up between the

mummy's arms. I held it against my chest and tried to open it.

My sweaty fingers slipped again.

Claire yanked hard at the mummy's shoulders. Too hard. A strip of cloth broke off in her hand, and she fell back.

The phone snapped open, and I punched 0.

The mummy froze.

Its fingers slid away from my throat. It took a step back and froze.

A buzzing, crackling sound rose from the phone.

Static.

I stared back at the mummy. It didn't move.

I glanced down at the phone.

The static kept crackling.

"Norm!" Claire shouted. "Run! Now's our chance. Run!"

I took a deep breath and shook my head. "No," I replied. "No more running. It's all over."

13

An hour later, Claire and I stood with our parents outside the pyramid. We watched as Cairo policemen took Ari and his boss, Dr. Martez, away.

"Please believe me," Ari pleaded with my parents. "We didn't mean any harm."

"Ari is right!" Dr. Martez cried as he walked between two policemen. "My Mummy-land Theme Park was going to be a wonderful tourist attraction. I spent years working on the mummies, putting in radio controls. I still don't understand what went wrong."

The police didn't pay any attention. They hauled the two men down the sandy path and into two waiting police cars.

As the cars roared away, Dad turned to me.

"How did you know how to control the mummies?"

"The mummies stopped moving when I turned on the cell phone," I explained. "At first I thought it was just a coincidence. But when it happened again, I realized they all must be electronically controlled. Once I saw that, I stopped panicking."

"But what made the mummies go after Ari and Dr. Martez?" Mom asked.

"I'm not sure," I said. "I'm just glad they did."

"I bet I know," Claire told me. "It must have been when you punched in all those numbers, remember? You probably messed up Dr. Martez's signals or something."

"Yeah!" I agreed. "I bet I reprogrammed the mummies."

"Thank goodness for that," Mom declared. She frowned. "But the cell phone still couldn't call out. So how did you get hold of the police?"

I laughed. "I didn't. Ari and Dr. Martez called the police! They thought the mummies were going to *kill* them!"

Mom shook her head. "What an adventure!"

Dad chuckled. "I don't suppose you two

want to go back on the pyramid tour so Mom and I can see it too?"

Claire and I glanced at each other.

"Sounds good," Claire replied. "It's very educational. You learn a *lot* about limestone."

"Sounds good to me too!" I exclaimed. "After *this* pyramid adventure, I *need* something totally boring!"

About the Author

R.L. Stine is the most popular author in America. He is the creator of the *Goosebumps, Give Yourself Goosebumps, Fear Street,* and *Ghosts of Fear Street* series, among other popular books. He has written more than 100 scary novels for kids. Bob lives in New York City with his wife, Jane, teenage son, Matt, and dog, Nadine.

GIVE YOURSELF

Goosebumps®

...WITH 20 DIFFERENT SCARY ENDINGS IN EACH BOOK!

R.L. STINE

$3.99 EACH

❑ BCD55323-2	#1	*Escape from the Carnival of Horrors*
❑ BCD56645-8	#2	*Tick Tock, You're Dead*
❑ BCD56646-6	#3	*Trapped in Bat Wing Hall*
❑ BCD67318-1	#4	*The Deadly Experiments of Dr. Eeek*
❑ BCD67319-X	#5	*Night in Werewolf Woods*
❑ BCD67320-3	#6	*Beware of the Purple Peanut Butter*
❑ BCD67321-1	#7	*Under the Magician's Spell*
❑ BCD84765-1	#8	*The Curse of the Creeping Coffin*
❑ BCD84766-X	#9	*The Knight in Screaming Armor*
❑ BCD84767-8	#10	*Diary of a Mad Mummy*
❑ BCD84768-6	#11	*Deep in the Jungle of Doom*
❑ BCD84772-4	#12	*Welcome to the Wicked Wax Museum*
❑ BCD84773-2	#13	*Scream of the Evil Genie*
❑ BCD84774-0	#14	*The Creepy Creations of Professor Shock*
❑ BCD93477-5	#15	*Please Don't Feed the Vampire!*
❑ BCD84775-9	#16	*Secret Agent Grandma*
❑ BCD93483-X	#17	*Little Comic Shop of Horrors*
❑ BCD93485-6	#18	*Attack of the Beastly Baby-sitter*
❑ BCD93489-9	#19	*Escape from Camp Run-for-Your-Life*
❑ BCD93492-9	#20	*Toy Terror: Batteries Included*
❑ BCD93500-3	#21	*The Twisted Tale of Tiki Island*
❑ BCD21062-9	#22	*Return to the Carnival of Horrors*
❑ BCD39774-5	#23	*Zapped in Space*
❑ BCD39775-3	#24	*Lost in Stinkeye Swamp*
❑ BCD39776-1	#25	*Shop Til You Drop...Dead*
❑ BCD39997-7	#26	*Alone in Snakebite Canyon*
❑ BCD39998-5	#27	*Checkout Time at the Dead End Hotel*

Scare me, thrill me, mail me GOOSEBUMPS now!

Available wherever you buy books, or use this order form.

Scholastic Inc., P.O. Box 7502, Jefferson City, MO 65102

Please send me the books I have checked above. I am enclosing $__________ (please add $2.00 to cover shipping and handling). Send check or money order—no cash or C.O.D.s please.

Name ____________________ Age ________

Address ____________________________

City ____________________ State/Zip ________

Please allow four to six weeks for delivery. Offer good in the U.S. only. Sorry, mail orders are not available to residents of Canada. Prices subject to change.

GYG

SCHOLASTIC